BITTERSWEET AND MAGIC

BITTERSWEET AND MAGIC

Short Stories by
ELISSA MATTHEWS

Copake Lake Press, 2024

Several of these stories have appeared in prior publications. I have updated a few of them, the rest appear in their original form. "Another Saturday Night": Originally published in *Meshuggah*, June 1994. "The Devil and Katrina Sue": Originally published in Aura Literary Arts Review, Vol 4 No 1, Winter 1997. "A Good Man": Originally Published in *QuibbleLit,* Issue 11, August 2023. "How to Catch an Elf": Originally published in *The Advocate,* Vol 11 No 2, April/May 1997. "Persistence of Memory": Originally Published in *Lilith,* Vol 21 No 2, Summer 1996. "The Rainy Season": Originally published in <u>Reader's Break, Literary Anthology, Vol 2,</u> 1996. "Saint Cecelia of Paramus": Originally Published in *Red Rock Literary Review*, Issue 47, Fall 2021. "Soliloquy": Originally published in Words of Wisdom, Vol 15 No 1, Summer 1995. "Teddy Bear Juice": Originally published in *Lost Balloon*, May 22, 2024. "The Three Gods": Originally published in *Art Times*, Vol 13 No 3, October 1996. "The Werewolf of Sander's Notch": Originally published in Wicked Mystic, Issue 22, October 1993.

DEDICATION

This book is dedicated to my family – extended, distributed, complicated, but always extraordinary.

My brothers and sister and sister-in-law and brother-in-law who cheered me on.

My cousins who listened, and then listened some more, and then recommended good books or dragged me to a museum or out to pick peaches when I was stuck and needed to talk out loud.

My parents, grandparents, aunts, and uncles who told the best jokes.

And most of all, to Kim, Ian, and Graham, who led, shared, and provided ongoing color commentary, making mine a life that continues to come alive with stories.

Contents

Introduction

I wanted to call my first book of short stories "Slow Learner" but Thomas Pynchon beat me to it. Titles are not part of the copyright of a book, so I could reuse the name, but getting mixed up with Pynchon doesn't seem like a good idea.

My problem with settling on an alternative title is that the stories I write come in two separate flavors – stories about the bittersweet ironies of life, and stories about the magical wonder all around us. In the end, the only thing that captured this split was simply to say it straight out: some of these stories are about the bittersweet, some of them are about the magic.

I'd like to tell you a little more about two of these stories – one of each type.

"A Good Man" is a story I personally love, and perhaps it is my favorite story. When I was in eighth grade my English teacher told us "never ever start a story with the word 'good' in the opening sentence. It's just so bland." Back then I was a quiet, rule abiding, homework on time, low-key kid; I was a 'good' kid. I was more than a little offended that the word so often used about me was considered bland. I determined to write a story that started with that forbidden word, just to reassure myself that *good* was *good*. Over the course of several decades this challenge kept popping up, and one day, mid Pandemic, the heart of the story arrived, and then the ending, and suddenly the story was complete (give or take a hundred rounds of editing). I hope you savor the bitter and the sweet as much as I do.

"Werewolf of Sander's Notch" is the first story I had accepted for publication, and for this I owe thanks to Elizabeth George, author of the Inspector Lynley mysteries. I was reading one of her books and was suddenly plunged into the reveal — childhood sexual abuse and pain. Wow, I thought, she writes with such incredible courage! If I could learn to bring that courage to the page, I would be a much better writer. I started right then with the story I was working on, and having amped up the intensity, it was accepted by all three of the publications I submitted it to. Let's hear it for courage.

And for the magic, the bitter, and the sweet!

Elissa Matthews
September, 2024

TEDDY BEAR JUICE

So last night I was imagining that I had lived my whole life and now it was over. I was saying goodbye for the last time to everyone I cared about, and then dying and being reunited with the people who died before me: my mother, my grandmother, my little brother. It was an exercise out of my inner child workbook, guidance for living in the now. Sometimes I have trouble living in the now. Tears were running down my cheeks, wetting the pillow, when Len came into the bedroom and said, "Hey, Peaches, you awake?" in his Come and Get It voice.

Let me tell you about Len. He always calls honey "teddy bear juice," because what else would you call the stuff that comes out when you turn a plastic teddy bear upside down and squeeze it? I laughed about it the first couple of times, but after fifteen years of marriage, now I just ignore him. In fact, cold honey can be damn hard to squeeze out of that stupid, sticky plastic bottle with the nozzle cap that always falls off or won't come off at all when you twist it. And no matter what I ask him to pick up at the store, he always forgets it and comes home with three bags of junk food instead, but he will never take a list because he is absolutely going to remember everything This Time.

He's getting a little bald, and a little pudgy, and I can't ride in his car for long because the smell of the cheeseburgers he thinks I don't know about makes me queasy. Whenever I need some help around the house — a lightbulb I can't reach or a heavy table moved, taking the kids to the doctor or calling the plumber or yelling at the plumber or paying the plumber — Len is out somewhere running some pointless errand.

But he doesn't gamble, and he has a decent job, and he shaves every morning, even on the weekend, because he knows his beard gives me a rash.

And the kids still shout "Daddy's home!" and run to him with big grins and open arms when he rolls his smelly old fast food clunker up the drive.

And his smile is still the most beautiful sunrise I've ever seen.

So last night he came into the bedroom and said, "Hey, Peaches, you awake?" in his Come and Get It voice, but when he saw me crying he wrapped his arms around me and held me without saying a word. I told him about dying, and he smoothed my hair and tucked the quilt around me, got into bed with me and just held me. Someday one of us will have to bury the other one.

In the morning, while I'm brushing my teeth and imagining I'm not getting older, Len grins at me in the mirror, winks and says, "You owe me one. I come to bed all horny and you pretend to be dead."

In the mirror the laugh lines around my eyes get just a bit deeper. "Talk to the butt," I say. I flip the bottom of my robe up at him, dart out of reach, and go downstairs to make his coffee and toast with teddy bear juice.

Saint Cecelia of Paramus

When Cecelia Kaufman's car rose thirty-seven feet (and four inches) above the surface of the Garden State Parkway, two miles south of the Paramus, New Jersey exit, many people wondered how a Jewish atheist had come to be honored with such a miracle.

She herself, hanging above the now stationary rush-hour traffic, was the first to wonder much the same thing. "What the hell did I do to deserve this?" were her precise words, once the initial panic had subsided.

She had been heading home from her job at Kreutzer Bio Labs, breeding hybrid pumpkins, mindlessly listening to chatter on the radio and wondering if she had enough time to wash her hair before her latest blind date showed up, when her car had lifted gently off the ground and floated upward, gliding to a halt the aforementioned thirty-seven feet (and four inches) above the ground.

There she stayed for three hours and twelve minutes; long enough for television crews, police, thousands of gawkers and the local branch of the FBI to arrive.

Oddly, Cecelia rather enjoyed that time. True, when the engine had first cut out and her wheels lost traction, her stomach had jumped and her palms had slicked with sweat. She had wrenched herself around, looking for the cause of her sudden change of direction, and by the time it occurred to her to open the door and jump out, she was too high to do so. But the floating was so gentle, so peaceful, that fear seemed irrelevant. So she sat back and enjoyed the view – watching the stalled traffic back up until it was out of sight – and wondered how long they would all be stuck there. She rolled down her window and peered down onto the crowd. "At least if I need to pee, no one can see me," she thought, eyeing the styrofoam coffee cup in the cup holder. She turned on her phone and left a message for her sister Jessie, a little surprised that she got service. Wasn't she, well, out of the service area? She couldn't think of anyone else she wanted to talk to, so she fired projectiles at angry birds. Just before the battery died she texted her blind date to say she'd gotten stuck in traffic and would have to cancel. She turned on the radio and listened to a few news stations, but all she could get were traffic reports about some massive backup on the Garden State Parkway.

Obviously some local science fiction anomaly had descended from who knew where, to capture her Chevy and hoist it aloft. She unbuckled her seat belt and waited for the miracle to give out, hoping her life would not end as a splotch of metal and flesh, two miles south of the Paramus Park Mall. "Before I die, it would have been nice to date just one guy, just one guy, who isn't a jerk." She sighed. She wondered if her sister Jessie would take care of her plants.

At 8:02pm, the car just settled back down as softly as it had lifted off. Cecelia leapt out even before the tires were solidly grounded, and one quick photographer captured her image that instant: leggy and disheveled and flinging long brown hair out of her face, thus forever associating the woman, rather than the car, with the event.

Amidst the tangle of police, first responders, journalists and gawkers, one reporter managed to lunge in next to her and stab a microphone into her face.

"Were you frightened?" the reporter had asked.

"Well a little, at first, but it was all so quiet and calm. After a while I realized all I could do was just wait it out."

"You could feel the Hand of God upon you."

Cecelia looked more closely at her interviewer, saw that the intensity in those questioning eyes was bordering on the "do not accept a ride from this person" level, and side-stepped away. "I don't believe in God," she said.

Eventually a police escort led her back to her apartment complex. She handled her car carefully, not quite trusting it. Dogged by reporters, she scuttled into her apartment, where she poured herself a tall scotch with very little ice, left another message for her sister Jessie, and turned off her phone. Her inbox was already full. She put a large sign on her door that said "Fuck Off" in black magic marker, then fell across her bed and crashed into sleep.

Jessie arrived an hour later, having battled her way through the cordon of reporters. When Cecelia opened the door to let her in, a reporter shoved in behind, wedging a shoe in the narrow gap.

Cecelia kicked at it as the reporter babbled questions.

Jessie stepped up and stared up at the reporter. "I'm Ms. Kaufman's attorney," she said calmly. "If you don't remove your foot, I will file trespassing and harassment papers." Then she quietly closed the door behind the retreating foot. Cecelia blinked. Jessie actually did look a little like a lawyer on a day off from the office, not the home appliance sales rep that she actually was.

By morning, the photo of her leap from the car had gone viral. It ultimately appeared on www.funz-funny.com site with the words "I don't believe in God," bubbling over her head, and the caption "The Flying None" below. By the end of the day it had 3,248,027,913 hits. Reruns of the 60's tv sitcom rocketed to the top of the NetFlix hit list.

"This better blow over soon," Cecelia said. "I already have a major headache."

"I think you're missing the big picture. People believe you worked an honest-to-literal-God miracle on prime time. This isn't going to disappear any time soon."

"Since when do you believe in God?" Cecelia asked.

"I don't," said Jessie. "But I can work with this. Selling miracles beats selling water softeners." She took a pad out of her briefcase and started making notes. Cecelia didn't think the event had anything to do with her, the situation made her curious. Maybe something good could come of this after all.

Soon Fox News was announcing that for the third week in a row, churches all over the country were crammed to capacity. They aired endless footage of Cecelia waving graciously to the crowd and walking with flowers in her arms. "Christ, I look like Princess Kate,"

"You're supposed to," said Jessie, who had taken over Command Central, as Cecelia had begun to call her apartment. "I've been very careful with your image. Non-partisan, non-religious, non-anything, really."

"Yeah, yeah, the Flying None. Well the None is bored. I've been cooped up all day with nothing but the occasional trek – wait for it - all the way down the stairs to the front door and back! Spiced up by the weekly raucous jaunt around the terminal ward at the children's hospital." She lit a cigarette, a new habit she was quite coming to enjoy. "My heart breaks for those kids. I hate those visits. I'd really like to get back to my pumpkins."

"Settle down, eventually the right offer will turn up."

"Like this one?" Cecelia turned her laptop around so

Jessie could read the screen. One conservative religious group was petitioning the Pope to canonize her.

Jessie sprayed coffee over the table as she laughed. "Saint Cecelia of Paramus? Really?"

"Thank God it takes three miracles to make a saint," Cecelia said, pointing to one of the comments below.

"And I think you have to be dead."

The next miracle began that very afternoon. A doughnut shaped cloud appeared in the sky, centered over her apartment building. The hole in the middle allowed a patch of clear sunlight to illuminate Cecelia whenever she left her apartment, with rain prevailing for seven tenths of a mile around.

Everyone, including Cecelia, stood in the parking lot and stared, openmouthed. People fell to their knees in the mud and started to chant her name. As Cecelia stepped forward the crowd surged, straining to touch her.

"This," said Jessie, standing in the rain, "is the chance we've been waiting for. Let's get packed, we're going to Zambia."

"Hey huh?"

"You've been complaining you want to do something. Well Central Africa needs rain."

"How do we know it will follow me?"

"I guess we'll find out. Either way, we'll get a fun trip out of it."

Jessie arranged private transport to the capitol city of Lukasa. The cloud followed them like a well-trained hound. Physicists and meteorologists raced to study the phenomenon.

"This is getting out of hand," Cecelia thought.

An entourage followed them. Every time she opened a browser or turned on her laptop, images of her were trending. Someone had dug out a copy of her high school yearbook. Cecilia refused to look, that haircut was just plain embarrassing. The more serious reports were trying to explain the phenomena as a miracle, a hoax, or mass hypnosis perpetrated by a secret cabal that had remained in power after the fall of the Soviet regime.

She alternately walked and drove slowly from town to dusty, starving town, trailing her pet cloud behind her. Everywhere she went, the best possible accommodations were prepared for her. Everywhere hands and eyes reached for her. Crosses were lifted up for her to bless. "I'm sorry," she repeated over and over, "I don't really do that."

Even more unsettling was the look she caught Jessie giving her once in a while. Jessie was starting to become one of the believers. The New Believers, they called themselves. Cecelia felt completely alone.

As a result of the new surge of press, Jessie now spent her time poring over resumes, looking for a speechwriter to prepare sound bites. She chose DeWayne Mariaus, who had crafted the award winning, wholesome-but-witty ads for Mama Genero's spaghetti sauce, and the award winning, ethical-but-entertaining ads for Big Tiger condoms. He had volunteered for the position because he truly believed that God was working through Cecelia and wanted little more than the chance to be near her.

"Schmuck," muttered Cecelia. He was cute, but he had the common sense of a cranberry.

"I believe we should work harder than we have been to settle our differences without violence," he penned for a visit to South Korea. "After all, no one looks good in bandages."

Statistics began to roll in: the fighting in the Crimea was tapering off. Attacks in the Israeli West Bank ended overnight. Even gang crime in Los Angeles was down.

"I believe we should try to face the problems of life and reality by turning to each other, not by turning away. Life, love, and rock'n'roll, people!"

He had originally written "my people," but Cecelia flatly refused. She did appreciate the way he consistently messaged that people try, just try.

Drug use dropped immediately. Alcohol and liquor sales were down the world over. Deadbeat fatherhood was out, visiting animal shelters was in.

"People just needed an excuse to be nice to each other," DeWayne said.

"He's a sap." Cecelia eyed Jessie's purse. "Where did you hide my cigarettes?"

"You can't smoke, you have to watch your image."

"Screw my image." When no one was looking she stole a pack from the Egyptian translator.

The donut cloud finally dissipated, leaving behind an awestruck planet and a mass migration toward zero population growth, green resource usage, and macrobiotic diets. Cecelia was ecstatic. The miracle was over, she could finally go home! She hadn't said anything, but this strange new life was taking its toll on her. Her day was filled with people begging: for salvation, for inspiration, for blessing. Her dreams were filled with hands, with eyes, with voices reaching out, grabbing and tearing pieces until there was nothing left.

"You still don't get it, do you?" Jessie shook her head. "You can't go home. This isn't your show, you're just the lightning rod. Where you go, it goes, and so do the crowds, and the attention, and the believers. People need to believe."

"In other words, I'm trapped. Forever." Cecelia stomped into the bedroom and slammed the door. "All I want before I die is to date one guy, just one guy, who isn't a jerk."

The Miracle Team continued to grow. Jessie was still in charge, DeWayne still led public relations, but now there were assistants to make travel arrangements and advisors on everything from public policy and government affairs to Oriental art and space technology. There was a chef and a personal trainer. The arguing was incessant, and Cecelia sometimes thought she would punch Jessie, when she opened her briefcase every morning at 8:02 and announced the day's agenda. How she longed for the clean solitude of her bio lab and being responsible for nothing more than the hybridizing vigor of her pumpkin seeds.

Jessie agreed with Cecelia on one thing – the less the world saw of her, the better. Cecilia had taken to snarling and swearing at nearly everyone, if not handled very carefully. She would stray from DeWayne's carefully worded statements, launching into her own belief that no God existed. When Prince Stephan of Castille presented her with his hypothesis that God looked on her as a challenge, she stabbed him in the leg with her salad fork. Privately the Miracle Team had begun to refer to her as Snagglepuss.

"Maybe we could get her a tranquilizer," someone suggested.

"Cecelia doesn't do drugs," Jessie snapped.

"I was thinking a tranquilizer dart, actually."

Several people snickered, but it was notable that no one actually laughed. Or disagreed.

"Maybe she needs a vacation."

"Yeah? Where can she go?"

"Maybe she should take up painting."

"Jogging."

"Maybe she needs to get laid."

"If it gets me out of the saint business, I would sleep with a yak," Cecelia said, when a carefully worded suggestion was made.

They picked a man in secret and vetted him completely, but he appeared in Cecelia's bedroom overlooking Lake Geneva with a bomb concealed in a body orifice. He was killed instantly when it detonated. The front wall of the chateau blew out, landing on the crowd, killing two and injuring four.

Several religious groups took credit for the attack, with Beware the False Prophet, Ltd. leading the way.

Cecelia was unharmed.

The world press announced a third miracle and the movement toward sainthood began to build up an unstoppable head of steam.

The second potential date was selected, vetted, stripped, searched, and x-rayed. He was completely clean, but when he tried to garotte her with the lamp cord, they rolled out of bed and he hit his head against the corner of the glass bedside table and died on the spot.

Cecelia was unharmed.

The Miracle Team tried to hush it up, but the Medical Examiner in Buenos Aires was a New Believer who felt it was his duty to share his faith, and his official report.

Someone digitized a halo into a photo of Cecelia and posted it on the New Believers website. It quickly became the first, and sometimes the only, image that came up in a search. It made Cecelia nauseous to even look at it, so she shut her laptop and refused to open it. World of Warcraft had so many healers name *RogueCecelia9675232* or *ElfCeeCee3627* she couldn't even escape to Pandaria. Her life had been reduced to library books and a deck of damp playing cards.

Four gunmen in Paris were turned in by friends while planning their attack. Three more bomb attempts were made: in Kenya, Ireland, and Laos, killing a total of twenty-three people, and a horse.

Cecelia stumbled and broke the heel on one of her favorite shoes.

"It truly is a miracle," murmured DeWayne in a hushed voice. "Lo though ye walk through the Valley of Death, ye are --"

Jessie and two of the other team members pulled Cecelia off him before serious damage was inflicted. Cecelia went into her bathroom and threw up, then leaned against the cool tile floor and cried.

Leaders from every nation clamored for Cecelia's attention. "It is an honor," said Pope Pius XLX, "for me to be in the presence of a living saint, Your Holiness."

"I can't think why," she replied. "You're the one that

hired me, so to speak. Your Holiness." The Roman Catholic Pontiff had risen to the top of the World Church, which had canonized Cecelia sometime around the third poisoning attempt.

"Please, call me Henri," he said. "It is an honor because you have brought God to us, to me." He was a young Pope, with a broad, strong peasant's build and a French accent.

"Oh yes? How so?" She realized his eyes were green. One didn't often think of the Pope in terms of eye color.

"You have made faith so much simpler, so much more joyous for so many." He leaned forward, his chin propped up in one hand, his gaze distant. "God is a fisherman, bringing us all into the grace of His net."

He really did believe, Cecelia marveled. He had no doubts at all. "God selected you because you don't believe in Him. He is showing us that faith is of the believer, not of worldly evidence."

"The last man who suggested that got the pointy end of a fork in his thigh."

"Ah yes, so I have heard." His smile was gentle. Forgiving.

She wanted to confide in him that all she really wanted was a date with a nice man, but she didn't think that would be, well, courteous. She bid him a rapid goodnight.

Alone in yet another hotel room, Cecelia stared at

herself in the mirror. Everyone was filled with the light of salvation except her. Everyone was in love, except her. World peace had finally occurred, and she still couldn't get a damned date. She couldn't even go home.

She turned away from the mirror in disgust and burst into flames.

"Oh hell, what now?" Her clothes curled into charred snow and flaked to the ground. She turned back to the mirror and watched the flames dance around her, up and down her arms and body, twisting through her hair. "DeWayne and Jessie are going to have a field day with a naked, flaming saint. A real challenge to their creative marketing skills." She laughed until she couldn't stand up, sinking to the floor in a heap, gasping for air.

Jumping back to her feet, she surveyed the singed outline of her buttocks in the roses of the carpet, surrounded by a dance pattern of grey footprints. She fled to the bathroom and climbed into the tub. Knowing it would do no good, she turned on the shower. The water hit her skin and skittered off, sizzling into steam then rising away. She reached out to turn off the lights, leaned back against the cold enamel and sighed. It was going to be a long miracle.

She tried to make herself comfortable in the hard tub. At least the flames had warmed it up. She looked up through the skylight over the tub. "I haven't slept in a bathtub since college, you know," she said to the dark sky.

"Is this the way you treat all your saints?" Stars stared silently back.

It would be so much easier if she really did believe, she thought. If she'd been caught by the faith, like all those others. Like DeWayne and Jessie. "You're wasting your time, you know. You keep throwing this shit at me, but faith is something you have, not something you decide to have." She curled her arms behind her head and fell asleep gazing at the silent ocean of stars.

The flames spun around her for a minute more, then quietly flickered out.

Inside Cecelia's dream, she could feel the return of the ordinary world.

Jessie took one look at her the next morning at breakfast and stopped reading. "There aren't going to be any more miracles, are there?"

"No, I don't think so."

"What happened?"

"I think God gave up on me."

"You don't believe in God." Jessie tipped her head and studied her sister.

"That doesn't mean he doesn't believe in me."

"Well, not if He's given up on you, He doesn't."

They both began to laugh at the same time.

Things were looking up already. She and Jessie were speaking the same language again, for the first time since practically the very beginning.

"I'm finally going home." Her whole body seemed to relax into that sentence.

"People still need to believe," Jessie protested.

"But on a sane schedule. With time off for good behavior."

"Ok, fine. We'll dial it back." As she did every morning, Jessie pulled a folder out of her briefcase and began to review the day's appointments. "Want to go to Pompeii after we bless the economists at the Université da Roma? DeWayne is bringing some archeologist to meet you."

"Sounds good." Cecelia poured another cup of coffee. "Maybe this one won't blow himself up. How soon will people get bored, now that I'm just ordinary again?"

"They'll never notice. Once a saint, always a saint."

DeWayne came into the room and kissed Jessie.

"Cecelia," DeWayne said, indicating the man at this side, "this is Roberto Saldana. He's currently studying the evidence of advanced agriculture in Roman civilization."

Cecelia looked up and found herself swimming in warm chocolate. He smiled. She smiled.

"Early attempts at pumpkin seed hybridization in the pre-literate culture." Roberto said.

"You're kidding, right? Pumpkin seeds?" He certainly was yummy, Cecelia thought. "Not Roman gods and goddesses? Early evidence of true faith?"

"Nah, I'm an atheist."

"Oh good," Cecelia said. "That's really, really good." She tried to look away, but she didn't try very hard.

One last miracle. The final worm a fisherman might throw into the water, no hook attached, at the end of a long and successful day on the water, a small tribute to the one that got away.

PERSISTENCE OF MEMORY

Whenever I see that picture of the clocks melting all over the place I think of my brother Izzie's wife Gitla and what happened to her. Her memories came up and practically bit her right in the *tuchas*. But that's what happens, isn't it? Inside our heads time rolls around like a ball of string, getting tangled in everything, and the memories you thought you had packed away in the back of the hall closet come tumbling out all over the floor one day when someone opens the door the wrong way, so to speak. But it was just a shame, what happened to Gitla.

It started with my nephew Herbie, Gitla and Izzie's boy. I knew first, but I didn't tell anyone. I maybe hinted a little to Izzie, but he told me I was crazy, so alright, I know when to keep my mouth shut. But I saw them. There I was, splitting a corned beef on rye with Ruth Feinberg in that deli on 87th, which is pretty good, only they give you too much sandwich for one and not enough slaw for two, when I saw the two boys in the booth in the very back corner. They were whispering and holding hands. With each other. And the thing is, the blond one is my nephew Herbie. Right away I think, "Uh oh, Gitla, you're not going to be a grandma any time soon."

"Don't look," I said to Ruth, but of course she looked. Thank heaven they didn't notice.

I tell Ruth, "Personally, I think live and let live. But Gitla is going to drop dead when she finds out. She's so..." I am hunting for a word to describe Gitla. When my brother first brought her home to meet Momma and Poppa, I didn't take to her at all. She was always in charge, making a big fuss over the dinner, making a big fuss over Izzie, making a big fuss over the wedding. And she always had to be right, no matter what. "Claire," she said to me, "if you fluff your hair up a little in front it would be much more flattering."

"I like my hair like this, it highlights my eyes."

"That's what I mean," she peered at me intently, "are you sure you want people to notice that your one eye is just a tiny bit smaller than the other?"

But Momma liked her. "She has a good heart," Momma said. "And she's strong, she'll be good for Izzie, she'll keep him in line."

After a while I got to like her too, but she still made a big fuss about everything and had to be right all the time. When I broke my arm she made enough food to feed Coxey's army and filled my kitchen. "You shouldn't be working, you should be resting," she told me. "And if you need anything else, you let me know, it's no trouble. And when you're back on your feet, I'll give you the name of my cousin's carpenter, he built the most beautiful cabinets for her kitchen, she had old ones just like yours."

I cannot explain this to Ruth. "She's one of the strong ones," I say, but Ruth gives me a look means she doesn't understand. Ruth was born in America, she didn't go to the camps. In the camps, you got so you could pick out the weak ones and the strong ones right away, without thinking it through with your brain. You didn't spend time with the weak ones unless they were family.

"They had homosexuals in the camps, too," I told Ruth. "They were brought in for re-education and right thinking." I shuddered. In some ways, that had been worse.

I peeked over at Herbie and his friend in their corner, without really looking, so they wouldn't see. Gitla was always *kvelling* about how handsome her Herbie was, with his blond hair and his great cheekbones.

"You should see all the girls chase him," Gitla said.

"I've fixed him up with Essie Miller, I think we're going to hear an announcement soon," Gitla said.

"He can choose any girl he wants, no wonder he can't settle down. I should only have been so good looking when I was a girl," Gitla said.

"He's studying to be a doctor," I tell Ruth. "He's studying with a cancer specialist at Sloan Kettering."

"He must be very smart," Ruth says politely, since Herbie is my brother's boy.

"By Gitla, he's Albert Schweitzer," I say, "but how smart can he be, holding hands with his boyfriend right here in Goldfarb's where anybody can see?"

And sure enough, wasn't I right? It was no more than two months later they did get caught. Of course I had to hear it from Charlotte Brodstein, who got it from her husband David, who got it from Izzie, who should have told his own sister first but he was so *meshuggah* from the whole thing he wasn't thinking straight. According to Charlotte, Gitla and Izzie were supposed to meet Herbie at his apartment and bring him a dinner, only Herbie forgot, and when Gitla and Izzie get there the boyfriend answers the door in his bathrobe.

"Hello," he says, "who are you?"

"We're Herbie's parents," Gitla says, "who are you?"

And just then Herbie comes skittering to the door wearing only his bathrobe, so even a blind cow with a headcold could tell what had been going on.

Right away Gitla starts to scream, "How could you do this to me? I raised you right! I raised you to be a good boy, I gave you love and I took care of you, and this is how you repay me?" And she drops the bag of dinner, Charlotte says, and the jar of borscht breaks and spills like blood on Izzie's shoes and most of the hall floor.

Then Herbie starts screaming, "Don't tell me how much you sacrificed for me. All you ever think about is yourself. No matter what happens to anyone else, no matter how hard something is for someone else, all that counts is how you feel, not how anyone else feels."

Then the boyfriend starts crying, "Please stop, you two, please don't fight about this. I can't stand it when people who love each other fight."

So she's screaming and Herbie's screaming and the boyfriend is crying and Izzie starts to feel his heart pounding, he has a weak heart, you know, he takes those little pills, and he leans against the wall to catch his breath and Gitla yells, "You see what you've done now, you're killing your father, that's what you're doing, you're ripping the heart right out of his chest." And she grabs Izzie and marches him down the stairs and drives him home.

"And then what happened?" I ask Charlotte.

"What should happen?" Charlotte says. She shrugs her shoulders up and down. "She'll start talking to him again sooner or later. She has to, she only has one son."

But I think to myself, she can be pretty stubborn, Gitla can. And Herbie, when it comes to stubborn, he's no slouch either. From the time he was a little boy, when he wanted something he would cross his little arms over his chest and just stand there with his bottom lip sticking out. He was the cutest little bug, going nose to nose with Gitla over turnips.

And more often than not he would win. She would heave a great sigh and throw her arms around him and laugh, with the dimples just like his coming out in her cheeks. "Alright then, you little *schmendrik*, go play. But tomorrow you eat your vegetables, you hear?" And he would give her a big kiss back, and all would be fine until the next fight.

Somewhere along the way, the kisses got lost and the only thing they have left is the stubborn.

After a while things mostly settled down, but Gitla still refused to speak to Herbie. She tried to get him banned from the family holidays but that didn't work. The first year she says to me, since Seder is always at my house, "If he's going to be there, so help me I will turn around and go home, take your pick, him or me." But Gitla's mother, may she rest in peace, who was still alive that year, 84 and as mean as the day she was born, God bless her, announced that since she only had a few years left to live, she was going to spend them with Herbie since she'd already put up with Gitla for 63. So Herbie kept coming to the family dinners, and Gitla kept not speaking to him, and we all got used to looking the other way and not getting too close if it seemed the fireworks were about to start.

But people can get used to anything, can't they, and after a while it starts to seem normal. Personally, I think this is what holds families together, they stop noticing how crazy things really are and start thinking it's the way things should be. So the fireworks didn't start on their own, they got pushed.

Gitla's mother died just before the new year but Herbie came to the Seder just like usual. Only this year, Herbie brings his boyfriend, the same one I saw in Goldfarb's that day, mind you. Things were a little tense, what with Gitla talking to everyone but the two boys, and being very obvious about it, and making lots of snide comments about abominations before God, especially on a holy night, and Izzie trying not to take sides, and the boyfriend talking about how everyone ought to hold hands, and the rest of the family trying to act normal, and in this family that's a tough job, even with a full wind behind and three horses pulling.

So we sit down to dinner, and after the service, which as usual runs a little too long, and what with all that wine, and the lamb and the turkey and the sweet potatoes with the little kosher marshmallows on top, and the matzoh and the honey cakes, and the macaroons and the marzipan, maybe a couple people aren't thinking so good. Nobody really notices at first that Gitla's sister Sarah is drinking a little more than usual. So maybe she starts getting a little drunk, and Gitla apparently has to say something, so she says, "You gonna keep drinking until you fall over, or you gonna stop one of these years?"

Sarah looks up, and she looks Gitla straight in the eye,

and she says, "Getting drunk is the only way I can put up with your shit. This is my family too, you know."

Gitla pulls herself up very straight at the table and looks at Sarah from her little eyes with just the eyelashes poking out. "I don't know what you're talking about," she says very slowly.

"Yes you do, Gitla." Sarah is shaking now. "You know what I'm talking about."

"No, Sarah, I have no idea what you're talking about." Gitla is biting off each word one at a time.

"Yes, you do." Sarah's hands are squeezing the napkin like she's going to tear it in half. "You've been treating Herbie like garbage for years now, and while Momma was alive I was going to keep my mouth shut, but you're getting worse, not better, and I'm going to put a stop to it right now."

Gitla has this frozen look like even her skin has been turned into stone, and she's sitting there, all the plates still on the table in front of her, and she doesn't say a word.

"You want to know how come your mother is so upset about you being a queer?" Sarah says to Herbie.

Herbie, who is no dope, even if he is Izzie's son, stares at his plate and doesn't say a word. The boyfriend is completely white, and he's for sure not looking at anyone.

Sarah looks around the table, her face stretched tight over her bones, and there isn't anyone who says a word to stop her. Sarah starts to speak at last, her voice low and fast. "I've let Gitla get away with this for too long already. You know why she hates you being queer? Because she thinks you got it from her."

In the heavy silence that follows this, I heard a moth beating its wings against the glass of the dining room window. "Who's ready for coffee?" I call out.

Gitla's shoulders and jaw were as stiff and as square as I had ever seen them. Dark, blood-stained patches were growing on her cheeks. "You are a fool, Sarah. You are a stupid fool." Her voice was high and tight.

"I was there, Git. She gave you that locket she managed to hide from the guards all those years."

"That's not true."

Sarah relaxed and got this sneaky mean look on her face. She'd spilled her dirt, now she was driving the wagon. "What was her name? Miriam? Marta? Ah yes, Maya." She took a sip of her wine and leaned back in her chair. "She was really beautiful, wasn't she, with her dark, gypsy eyes and her red, red lips. And the way she used to laugh, I can still hear her. It frightened me when she laughed, that someone might hear." In the silence around the table Sarah's small chuckle rang loud. "You still have that locket in your jewelry box. I saw it there when I put back the pearl earrings I borrowed that time."

"That's not true." Gitla's voice was still and calm

enough to freeze cream, but her face was flushed dark and blotchy under the thick skin. Sarah turned to Herbie and leaned forward across the table. "You know what happened to Maya? After the war, she married a man, and your mother stayed in bed and cried for three days."

A low sound started. It didn't sound like it was coming from Gitla, not at first. It sounded like it was coming from the room in back of her, or the closet, it was so low and hollow. It was a sound that ran right through your bones, and only when it got louder did I realize it was Gitla, screaming, screaming so deep down inside that it echoed like a train in a tunnel. And it got louder, and louder, and louder, a train rushing closer from a long, long distance away, until the children put their hands over their ears, and even the silverware began to jiggle a little. She didn't seem to need air to breathe, she was just screaming without moving a muscle. Then she leaped out of her chair, knocking it over backward with a crash and smashing her hands down on the plate full of gravy and potatoes. "That's not true!" she screamed in that same train rushing, thundering voice. Then the sound stopped with a suddenness like a bang, and she ran from the table, out the door to the street, slamming it behind her.

Izzie looked around at us all, his face blank and lost. "Go after her," I said quietly, "she needs you now." And he, too, disappeared out the door. I wondered what Momma would have thought.

After the door shut behind him, we all just sat there, not looking at each other, not saying a word. I tried to think of something to say, but I couldn't. It didn't seem to be the right time to pour coffee.

Finally Herbie coughed. His boyfriend sat slumped in his chair, ashen grey. He looked old and tired. I suppose we all did, a little. "Why did you do that, Aunt Sarah?" Herbie asked.

She turned to him slowly with tears running down her sunken cheeks. "At the end of three days, the sister I had loved with all my heart, who dragged me, barely alive, through four years of hell, my sister was gone and that stranger came to take her place." With a single, fierce movement she picked up her wineglass and flung it at the wall where it shattered into little pieces, leaving a broad arc of wine behind. "I wanted to hurt her, God damn it!" Then she too ran out the door into the night. Thin lines of purple trickled down through the blue flowers on the wallpaper.

After that everyone else left, saying quiet goodbyes. Misha and I cleared away the dishes and cleaned up the mess. "Gitla will start talking to Herbie again now," Misha said. "To save face."

"I know. But it won't be the same." I scrubbed at the big blotch on the dining room wall.

"That stain won't come out," he said, watching me

scrub. "We'll have to put up new wallpaper."

"It was time for new paper," I said, putting the sponge away. "Ruth Feinberg has almost the same pattern in her dining room, and I was getting tired of it anyway." I sat down in one of the empty chairs and the waves of tired rolled over and over me, like they had in Buchenwald. I just wanted to lie down, shut my eyes, and sleep.

A Good Man

He was a good man. Everybody said so. He taught woodworking and knot tying to the Boy Scouts, even after his own two boys were long gone to college. Good schools, both of them. He shoveled the snow from his walk without paying attention to stopping exactly at the property line, and shoveled the walk for Tessie Barks the winter she broke her arm in a fall on the ice. He religiously bought lemonade from any summer stand, no matter if the cups – or the child selling it – were slightly grubby. He didn't fondle co-workers of either sex, and he never took credit for ideas or sales that weren't his. He was inordinately patient about repeating things for his wife, who seemed to be a bit hard of hearing, or absentminded, or something. Nobody knew for sure. Everyone smiled when they saw him, and he smiled back, always stopping to talk if there was time and apologizing if there wasn't.

He was just as good a man behind closed doors. He didn't drink. He didn't smoke or snort cocaine, he didn't download pictures of teenage Serbian prostitutes. His children never had to wear long sleeves or calamine lotion and tell the teacher they had poison ivy. There was no one locked in his basement, or his attic – in which all the seasonal decorations were boxed and labeled - or behind a secret panel in the back of the tool shed at the end of his vegetable garden. He did more than his share of the chores, gently tucked a blanket around his wife if she fell asleep on the couch while he was talking about his day, and when he got angry he counted to ten, or walked away until he felt able to discuss the issue reasonably and rationally. He swam at the Y every day, and never even noticed if anyone else gained weight.

I first encountered him in the grocery store one afternoon shortly after my wife and I moved into town. He was ahead of me in line with his boys, who were probably 5 and 8 at the time.

"One candy bar to share," he told them.

"I want that one," the younger boy shouted.

"Inside voices," he said.

"I hate peanuts," the other shouted in a whisper. "I want caramel coconut."

"Noooo!" the younger one wailed.

"We don't have all day," the cashier snapped. "There's a line."

"I'm so sorry," he said, smiling at the cashier, then smiling at me. He picked up one of each candy bar, put them on the belt with the rest of the groceries, and then turned to the boys. "You will decide which one to share today, and which one will go in the cabinet for tomorrow."

Just like that, the boys settled down and started negotiating.

The cashier rang up the goods while he bagged them.

"I certainly hope you're paying cash," the cashier announced when the bagging was complete. She stabbed a finger at the sign by her head. "This is a cash only line."

"I'm happy to pay cash."

"I'd appreciate exact change as well."

"I don't have it, I'm sorry." He handed her the bills.

She glared at them, then put the money in the till. The register showed 78 cents return, but even from where I was standing I could see she had shorted him.

He looked at the money in his hand.

She slitted her eyes at him.

"That's not the right change," the eight-year-old said.

"Yes it is," the cashier said.

"There's a quarter coin not enough," the little boy said. "We learned coins in school."

"Then your father must have dropped it. I certainly didn't."

"But…"

The man put his hand on the boy's shoulder and cut him off. When he put the money carefully in his pocket without a word, it didn't feel like a gesture of weakness, of acquiescence to a bully, it felt like an act of generosity, of donating that quarter to someone who needed it more.

He smiled at the boys, at the cashier, at me, and walked away.

I bought my bread and roast beef, then overtook them just at the exit where he was crouching down with his arm around the older boy, who was sniffling.

"But she was so mean to me."

"I know."

"I was right. I can do coins."

"I know."

"Why was she so mean to me?"

He paused for a minute, and I did too, pretending to be reading the flyers for pet sitters and house painters on the bulletin board. "Sometimes even grownups can be mean, a little bit. You never know what's going on inside someone else's head. Or maybe her feet hurt. Wouldn't that make you a little crabby? It would make me crabby."

Both boys nodded, and the older one wiped his nose on his sleeve.

I hoped I would be as good a father in my turn.

One crisp October morning after the boys had grown and moved away, his wife of twenty-eight years ditched her job and her cell phone, climbed aboard a gleaming black Harley with scarlet flames that matched the new ink on her bicep, and was last seen heading west on Highway 10.

THE DEVIL AND KATRINA SUE

Katrina Sue floated slowly up from sleep like a bubble of air rising through warm syrup. She stretched her naked limbs against the damp sheets and inhaled deeply without opening her eyes.

"That was nice," the Devil murmured.

"Mmmm." Katrina rolled onto her back to let the air wash over her. Sweat trickled down to pool between her round breasts, in the hollow beneath her ribs, in her navel. Her long hair lay tangled and loose against the pillows. She felt refreshed and relaxed, as if the whole world were resting along with her.

"You are so beautiful, so unbearably beautiful," the Devil said, sliding one black-nailed hand down the silk of her thigh. His ebony eyes roamed over her, the animal slits narrowed with intensity. "I want you to be mine. You will be my greatest triumph, the envy of Heaven and Hell."

"Mmmm." Katrina inhaled again, her red lips just slightly parted.

"Doesn't it mean anything to you that I lust for you

like this? Doesn't it move you at all to know you are the most beautiful woman born in three hundred years?"

Katrina opened her eyes and looked calmly at her glowering bedmate. "From you, such compliments mean nothing." She smiled gently to tell him she meant no insult.

"Because I am the Prince of Lies?" the Devil demanded. "I would have you know, this is no lie."

"It might be a lie, it might be the truth." Katrina rolled one perfect shoulder in disinterest. "Since I don't believe in you, it hardly matters what you think."

The Devil rolled onto her, his black nails grasping her arms, his body pressing down onto hers. He rasped the bed with his hooves and swished his tail. The forked end caught briefly on the blanket. "How can you not believe in this?" His hips arced forward. "Or this?"

"It's not your masculinity I doubt," Katrina said, stroking her hands absentmindedly across the sweaty skin of his chest. "It's your divinity that's in question."

"If I prove that I exist, will you be mine?"

"Will you make me the richest woman in the world?"

"Yes, yes," he agreed.

"And the wisest?"

"Yes, and again yes." His nostrils flared.

"And will I live a long and happy life, dying content at the age of one hundred and two, with generations of my children and my children's children around me?"

The Devil leaned forward, the light of victory in his eyes. "All this and more will be yours, Oh Lovely One."

"I'll think about it." Katrina patted Satan lightly on the arm and laughed.

The Devil bounced off the bed, his skin steaming, and towered over her. "You think you can play with me with impunity!" he snarled. "You think can look innocent and chaste and then make a fool of me. I will show you how wrong you are!" He wrapped his fingers around her wrist and yanked her to her feet. "I do not need permission to take your soul!"

Before them arose the Torments of Hell. Souls, legion upon legion, surrounded them, screaming in agony, writhing as they died, yet rising to die again. Demons stared at them from every corner of the realm. The Devil spread his arms wide and his unholy glee echoed around them. "You see before you my victories," he roared. "You see before you my triumphant and terrible dominion!"

"You are Lord of all this?" Katrina asked.

"Yes," crowed the Devil. "I am Lord! And now you are mine as well, my greatest prize!"

Katrina looked at all the agonies displayed before her. The light of dancing flames scattered gold flecks across her naked skin; lovely lines crossed her brow. She raised her eyes to his. "Set them free."

The Devil froze mid-laugh. "Say what?"

The other demons stopped to eavesdrop.

"If you are truly Satan, and if you truly want me more than any other, set those souls free."

"I cannot do that!"

"But you are the Lord of all Evil."

The demons started to giggle.

"Well, I don't want to do it."

"Then take me home."

"This is not a date!" Satan turned in fury. "This is Eternal Damnation."

Demons all over Hell laughed. The Devil flushed.

Katrina waited patiently, her gaze level and calm. "If there really is a Hell, I will trade my soul only for the souls of all others. Take it or leave it."

"You cannot set conditions before the Prince of Darkness." But he looked around him before he spoke.

"I don't believe in you."

Amidst a multitude of choking guffaws, one small demon fell over, holding his stomach, legs kicking the air.

The Devil slashed his arm upward and returned them to Katrina's bed. Katrina settled herself comfortably against the pillows, the edge of the sheet just covering the rose tips of her breasts.

"It occurs to me," she said, "that if there really were a Devil, he wouldn't waste much time on those already doomed, he must have bigger challenges." Her bright eyes laughed into his black ones. "Either you don't exist, or I'm going to Heaven in spite of you."

The Devil stomped to the window, his hooves striking sparks as he went. "You are infuriating! You know nothing of theology, or philosophy, or just plain logic. And the worst part is, you really believe what you're saying."

"I'm sorry," Katrina said, hiding a smile. "I didn't mean it."

"I'm leaving," he snarled.

"Will you be back tonight?"

"No."

"Well, this is goodbye then." Katrina held out one soft hand, but the Devil ignored it.

"Goodbye," he spat, and disappeared with his usual flash and swirl.

Katrina wrinkled her nose at the odor of sulfur that lingered in the air. He would be back, of course, with renewed wiles and even more sophisticated arguments. After all, she still did not believe in him.

SOLILOQUY

At the age of thirty-two, Louisa decided it was time to give up her virginity. She had not held onto it out of morality, nor was she waiting for true love, and it certainly was not from lack of opportunity. For unfathomable hormonal reasons men were greatly attracted to her large breasts, a phenomenon she had puzzled over endlessly as a teenager. Why were lumps of fat in one place so much more attractive than lumps of fat somewhere else?

No, the problem was, giving up her virgin status meant giving up, however temporarily, her carefully and comfortably arranged solitude.

But lately the critics were saying her poetry lacked passion and courage. Once they had talked about her potential, her insight, her satirical talent, and she had believed them. She let them teach her to hunger for more. She had a daydream she indulged in, only once in a while, about a packed reading, maybe in the library of a small and exclusive literary club, for the most illustrious names in all of time. She could smell the mildew on the rows of leather books behind her, and even in her imagination her fingers trembled as she turned the pages in front of her, in front of these literary faces so famous and so familiar.

But now the critics said she lacked passion.

Louisa studied the literature and literary criticisms. Certainly the sexual act, particularly the deflowering of the virgin, was an event celebrated in poem and play throughout every era. The most moving, the most exuberant language was reserved exclusively to describe the act of intercourse. "How odd," she said. But in idle moments her mind addressed the problems of arranging the event in such a way as to avoid ongoing impingement on her life.

She chose the man carefully. Not a stranger from a bar, considering the violence and disease rampant in this decade. Nor worse yet someone known to her, someone frequently encountered in the course of daily movements who would linger in the corners of her life. Louisa chose a married man of casual acquaintance who would be as glad to disavow all knowledge of her after the act as she would be to disavow him.

In the long, silent hours before dawn, as Louisa lay awake in bed deciding whether to arrive early at her dreary day job or go back to sleep, the prospect of what she was contemplating would descend upon her, and she would shudder with some unnamed emotion. Was it fear? Perhaps a little. Was it excitement and passion? Perhaps a little. Louisa struggled to decide, but in the end her mind scurried away from the loss of control such emotions implied. Jittery, she would quickly rise and shower, stuffing these thoughts out of reach.

When the time came, she set the stage with precision, returning to her research for direction. She bought vegetables fresh that morning from the farm market, picking through the mushrooms like a housewife from the old country, selecting only the smallest, the whitest, the roundest. She chose the plumpest chicken and bought a good burgundy for the sauce. Each pearl onion was tiny and perfect, waiting in its paper dress for its cue.

Then she cleaned the apartment. She felt it was important that the setting also be as close to perfect as she could make it, so the passion she sought would not be diluted. Sympathetic magic, really. She dusted and vacuumed every inch of flat surface, every hidden corner and crenelated molding. She washed the windows until they sparkled like an advertisement for ammonia, scrubbed the bathroom and polished every wooden table and chair with lemon oil. The scent lingered. She put Michael Bublé on the speakers, turned him up loud, and sang along as she skated through her preparations. When the old crab downstairs banged on the ceiling, she banged back and ignored her. "Go to hell, bitch," she muttered.

He came through the door and dripped rainwater on the freshly waxed floor. He dropped his wet coat over the arm of a chair and pulled her against him. "Hey, babe, I'm not hungry. At least not for food." His lips sought hers and his hands targeted her breasts. "How about we go straight to bed?" He had assumed, she realized, that her invitation meant exactly what it had indeed meant. His haste left her no time to give in to the sudden wash of nerves.

The lambently lit bedroom invited them, the soft layers of blanket enfolded them, naked skin slid against naked skin. His breath in her ear was hot and his hand sliding down the curve of her waist made her wriggle closer, watching his face in the dim light. The naturalness of their intimacy astonished her. There was very little pain, a growing pleasure, and a great deal of sweaty rocking as they locked inside and around each other.

Something huge and fiercely glittering began to grow, just out of sight. Yes, yes! Poetry lived there in fire and flame. Songs were born and raised glorious voice. The sonnets began to make sense: two hearts seared into one. Passion rolled toward her carrying eternity in its wake. She stretched for it and just as it skimmed her fingers, just as it surged up in the fullness of its immensity and glory, reaching out to engulf her, she covered her face and turned away. When she looked again it was gone and she moaned in regret.

Afterward he fell asleep and Louisa wrapped herself in a robe and slipped into the kitchen. She dished the uneaten dinner into plastic containers and made herself a cheese sandwich. Was she changed? Well, she was more conscious of her body sitting on the hard kitchen chair. Was there more passion in her than previously? Yes, of course there was. Wasn't there? She struggled to capture the cooling memory of fire.

All in all, she was as satisfied with the result as one can ever be with reality; her work was sure to benefit. Perhaps she would take a break from writing for a while and concentrate on her day job. Just a little while. The last embers of passion faded to black. She ate her sandwich and wished that man would wake up and leave.

Still Life, With Baby

W e should have a child," Marshall said.

Galip, relaxing, was caught off guard. The quiet of the evening was settling in, nighttime crickets and frogs singing in the summer air, the occasional car engine churning up the hill in the distance, a light wind tapping the twig ends of tree branches against the house. Galip raised his thick, black eyebrows in theatrical surprise and lowered his book. "Excuse me, I know I'm not a doctor, but we are missing something, yes? Like an X chromosome? And one of those incubator thingies? What are they called? Uteruses? Uteri?" After many years of practice, his Turkish accent was still noticeable at times.

"Yes, very funny." Marshall reclined against the corduroy sofa and spread his arms out along the back. With his pale hair ruffled and the light from the summer sun, setting late, creating shadows under his cheekbones, he was the Hollywood archetype of a Viking. Galip marveled that someone like Marshall could love someone like him – a swarthy little Turk with no social skills and a degree in library science. A dusty college librarian. Forty-two years old and as important as he was ever going to be.

"I know we haven't talked about this in a long time," Marshall said.

"Not since dating. We agreed children weren't right for us."

"That was a long time ago. Before we were married. Before we were settled."

"What's changed?"

"Our circumstances."

"I need to think about this," Galip said.

Marshall extended his long legs and placed one ankle on top of the other, smoothing the crease at his knee with two fingers. "A child would be so fulfilling. And we are eminently suited to raise a civilized human being. Lord knows the world needs a few more of those."

Galip inhaled to a count of four. "It's a big step. I am just not, um, sure we're ready."

"We're over forty, we're financially stable. A child would bring a new depth, a new texture to our relationship. We would be a family."

The look on Marshall's face, the way he breathed the word *family,* told Galip the real story. This was about Marshall's father. Maybe Marshall had seen him in town. Maybe they'd passed on the street, Marshall as hopeful as a puppy, his father steaming past without even a nod. "Your father will not welcome you back if we become a 'real' family," Galip said. Certainly a child would not appease his own father's rage.

"This is not about my father. This is about us," Marshall said. But he turned to the window, which reflected a dark and distorted image of the cozy living room back at them.

"He thinks you're an abomination. You said that yourself." Galip tried to take the sting out of his words with a sympathetic tone. "Are you still trying to prove to him how normal you are?"He studied Marshall intently, hoping he'd said the right thing, or at least said the wrong thing carefully enough.

Marshall sat up and thrust his chin forward. "I have nothing to prove to my father," he said. "Nothing."

Heaviness spread through Galip's chest. He felt so weighed down when Marshall refused to face the truth. When they'd first started dating fifteen years ago, there had been hope of reconciliation between Marshall and his father, or more precisely, Galip had not yet realized there was no hope. Marshall had become a lawyer, just like his father. He'd joined a law firm in the small Indiana town he'd grown up in, just like his father. He'd married a librarian, just like his father. Galip bent forward and gripped his knees. "You're always trying to measure up to him. And every time you do, you turn from me and go chasing after an illusion."

"Wanting a child is as much a biological imperative for men as it is for women."

Galip jerked back, slapped by Marshall's detour. "Oh, that's a good one," he said. "Your biological clock is ticking so you need the fulfillment of a few dirty diapers."

"Now you're just being childish."

"Then you sure as hell don't need a second one, do you?"

"You know I can't focus on your words when you raise your voice."

Galip leaped to his feet, the forgotten book falling to the floor with a thud. "As far as I'm concerned," he said, even louder, "the only advantage of being stuck out here in middle of nowhere, miles from anything but the damn chipmunks, is that I can make all the noise I want."

"Then go ahead and yell, darling. I'll be in the study." Marshall rose and stalked regally out of the room.

As soon as he was out of sight, Galip slumped back into the chair. *We need to get out of Chipmunkville.* He looked out the window at the darkness, the barely visible trunks of old trees, the echoing lack of human presence. *We need to belong somewhere. We can't keep hanging in limbo twelve miles down the road from your father, hoping he wakes up in a forgiving mood one morning. I need somewhere to belong, Marshall, and you keep pushing me away.*

He pushed himself to his feet went to bed.

Marshall slid in next to him much later. Sleepily Galip woke as Marshall reached out for him. "I'm sorry, darling," Marshall said. "I didn't mean to drop this on you like a bomb. A child is something we should decide together, not something to come between us."

"Mmmhmm," mumbled Galip, curling backward into Marshall's warmth.

"I do love you," Marshall whispered, as Galip faded back to sleep.

It was many weeks later when Galip realized they were no longer arguing about whether to have a child but had moved on to assessing methods of adoption. *Is this what I want?* Part of Galip hoped the state bureaucrats would block a middle-aged, gay couple from adopting, regardless of what the law said. A private adoption was still a possibility, of course, but that would present its own obstacles.

And then Marshall lit on the idea of artificial insemination and a surrogate mother. A child carrying Marshall's actual, familial DNA.

"You're nuts!" Galip gaped. How had Galip missed this obvious possibility? "You're out of your tiny, blond mind!" He was so astounded he couldn't even pace. He jittered into the kitchen, filled two large pots with water, and set them boiling on the stove, just to have something to do. He stood and stared as tiny bubbles formed and burst, growing larger.

I should leave.

But I love him.

I should leave.

But he loves me.

Without him I'd be nothing at all.

"Why did you do that?" Marshall asked sometime later, swimming through the damp mist that now filled the kitchen.

"I don't know," Galip said. "It just seemed to be called for." *Because you're not hearing me.*

"I think you're overreacting. After all, if we're going to have a child, what difference does it make whether we adopt or create one of our own?"

Because it wouldn't be ours, Galip wanted to say. It would be yours, and some woman's, and you would spend your life trying to give it to your father. The man who can't see how much courage it takes for Marshall to face old friends and neighbors who insist on saying "but you were the captain of the football team."

He turned to the stove and added salt and pepper to the gallons of boiling water. At least soup was something he could influence.

Galip knew he should have put his foot down when Celina

arrived. Marshall dropped her into their world the same way he did everything — she simply appeared on the doorstep one evening, framed against the backdrop of the ripe corn in the field across the road.

"Galip, this is the woman who has agreed to carry our baby." Marshall stood proudly next to her. "Celina Mariha Kuratowski."

The woman posed, petite and self-possessed, in the middle of the living room, a subtle smile curving her lips as she surveyed her new surroundings – the cozy, warm cottage, a calm haven to raise a child. Or was it the artwork, the antiques, the leather-bound books? Was she paying particular attention to Marshall's collection of jade figurines? In the overhead light, her pale honey hair shone as if lit from within. She looked, Galip realized, like Marshall's mother. *Of course she does.*

Galip could not unscramble his thoughts enough to speak. He wanted to make a scene: to yell and throw things and fight back, to oust this intruder on her perky little ass. He wanted to stalk off in silence and let Marshall do whatever he pleased with whomever he pleased. A horrible thought slunk forward. Was Marshall thinking about having sex — actual skin-on-skin intercourse — with this woman, not artificial insemination? He wanted to run to the bathroom and vomit.

Marshall took Galip's silence as victory. "I'm glad

you're not angry. I told Celina it could go either way."

Galip felt Marshall's tinny words plinking into him and bouncing off.

Celina stared at them, as placidly expressionless, as if she were watching a silent movie.

Marshall continued, oblivious to Galip's rigid silence. "It was easier than I thought it would be. I put an ad on a reputable surrogate forum, just to test the waters, as it were. But one look at her picture and I just knew she'd be the one for us."

"How long," Galip asked, moving nothing but his lips, "have you been interviewing women?"

Celina continued to stand nearby, calm and quiet.

Marshall stopped smiling. "Not long, really, not long at all." He rubbed his jaw. "You're angry, aren't you?"

"Yes." Galip unstuck his feet from the rug and clumped up the stairs. He would pack a bag and leave tonight. There was no relationship left in this relationship.

Marshall followed him. Galip's decision shimmered in the air between them, but Marshall stepped through it, putting his arms around Galip and gazing down, blue eyes into brown. "I know this is hard for you. I know I want this more than you do, and I shouldn't have gone ahead without you the way I did. But I appreciate you all the more for your generosity. No one — not the baby and certainly not a woman who will be around for a while and then disappear

— no one is more important to me than you are."

Galip rested his cheek against Marshall's chest and sighed. It was bullshit, but it was such welcome bullshit. When he was reminded so clearly that the distance between his love for Marshall and Marshall's love for him was achingly vast, the pain of it was like his bones being torn from their sockets. He had loved Marshall since the day they'd met. The way he forged ahead without letting anyone stop him. The way his strength brought out the best in Galip. The way Marshall held him when he teetered on the brink of self-loathing. Whenever he looked at Marshall's paycheck and then his own. Whenever he looked at Marshall's philosophy books, his art, his photography, and by comparison Galip went into the kitchen to cook a perfectly acceptable dinner, and settle down to read a perfectly acceptable novel.

When Marshall said he was important, Galip could pretend it was true. He *had* to pretend it was true. Without Marshall he could only return to the city and start over. At his age. With his looks. With all his fears and frailties. *I can do it if I have to, but oh, I do not want to.*

Celina moved into the guestroom after the contract was signed, and the insemination took hold on the first try. At first Galip objected to Celina living with them, but Marshall would not be persuaded. "She's the mother of our child. She can't live in a crappy apartment in that part of town." He trembled with the quiet intensity of his feelings. "Our child," he repeated.

Celina came with a laptop, two suitcases, and an alien attitude toward life that mystified and repelled Galip. She said that all she wanted out of the deal was money but Galip found himself watching her. She was twenty-eight and had no husband, partner, or plans that would interfere with her donating close to a year of her life portaging someone else's child around inside her, and then sticking around to nurse. She worked a remote job and had a flexible schedule. She would go to whatever doctor Marshall chose, deliver in whatever hospital Marshall selected, breastfeed for as many months as Marshall dictated, then disappear without a word. She was intelligent enough — she spoke, Galip found to his surprise, five languages. But Galip failed to discern any personality at all.

"So you're a Russian translator," he began one morning in the kitchen as she was sipping the protein shake Marshall had mixed for her before he'd left for work. Why did she need the money from this surrogacy if she already had a decent job? "That must be interesting, all that poetry and passion."

Celina half-shrugged without looking up. "I work on engineering textbooks and mathematical papers."

"That sounds so dry. Why don't you switch to

something else?"

She did look up then, her blue eyes as flat as a crayon circles. "I don't want to," she said.

Every conversation Galip tried to start seemed to end up the same way.

"Have you read this book?"

"No, I don't read much fiction."

"What did you think of that movie?"

"I fell asleep in the middle."

"Did you do anything interesting last night?"

"I went to the mall and looked at stuff."

"Oh, that is interesting," Galip forced himself to say. "Did you buy anything?"

"No. I'm okay with what I've got." "She's learning Turkish so she can talk to you in your own language," Marshall confided one night when Galip had been complaining more bitterly than usual. "But don't tell her I told you, she wants it to be a surprise."

"Even in Turkish I wouldn't have anything to say to that woman." Galip thumped his head onto the pillow. "She has no life in her except a fetus that happened to attach itself to her womb."

Fall slipped into winter; winter dribbled into an early, muddy spring. As Celina grew larger, the house seemed to shrink. Every flat surface held a book on pregnancy and babyhood that Marshall had bought and insisted Galip and Celina read, in addition to the videos and clips he emailed several times a day. Old appliances on the kitchen counter shuffled back into the corners as bottle warmers and trays of vitamins and minerals moved in. Taped lists festooned the cabinets: best foods for soon-to-be moms, top ten foods with folic acid, fruits and vegetables ranked from most to least toxic. Everywhere Galip turned he banged into rounded, pastel edges of baby paraphernalia. Everywhere Galip turned, the rounded curves of Celina sat, waiting and growing. Galip studied her, slurping her morning protein shake. She was wearing a set of the dark pants and floppy pastel shirts that made up her entire wardrobe. He'd heard that pregnancy made some women glow, and it was certainly true for Celina. She was practically iridescent. Underneath the shirt, her stomach bulged against the edge of the table. He turned away.

Marshall's mother came over three days in a row, breaking her routine of secret monthly visits to help transform the guest room into a nursery. Galip had always felt sorry for her, caught between her husband's rages and having to sneak around to visit her only son. Galip wondered if her husband ever hit her. She was so meek, perhaps he didn't have to.

"Call me Alma," she told Celina as they huddled with

Marshall over a book of paint swatches and wallpaper borders, three honey blond heads, three long necks bent like swans over the rainbow of colors, three pairs of hands with long, tapered fingers pointing and selecting. Galip stood by and watched. "Not knowing the sex makes it harder," Alma said.

"We want to be surprised," Marshall said. "I like the forest green, with the leaf print border."

"This is a nursery," Alma said, "not a reading nook."

"Then how about the mauve with the gold feathers?"

"It's also not an antique store."

In the end, they chose a sea-foam aqua with hummingbirds on the border. It was, to Galip's surprise, Celina's favorite color. This was the most personal thing he knew about her, Galip realized.

Alma caught his eye and smiled. As she was leaving, she pulled him aside. "When the dust settles, you and Marsh will go back to life as usual. With a baby, of course. Babies change things. But you'll find a new normal."

He glanced over his shoulder at Celina and Marshall standing together in the kitchen.

"Celina will leave when the baby comes," Alma said.

The contract stated that when the breastfeeding months were over, Celina would take her money and go. Then the baby would belong only to him and Marshall. "What if she doesn't?"

"She will. Marshall needs you. He's just like his father."

On the day of the baby's arrival, Galip was shocked by the strength of the emotions that seized him right from the beginning. A hurricane bore down on him, and he went with it. A baby. His baby. He paced in the waiting room of the hospital, as terrified and eager as any new father. *I'm going to be a father.* Marshall was in the delivery room, and Galip wanted to be there as well, but visions of gory birth fluids had scared him away. He perched on the gray vinyl couch, stuck his finger into a hole in the fake fabric, and tugged, waiting.

At long last a nurse came to fetch him. "Mom and baby are doing just fine; it all went smooth as silk."

It may have gone easily for a birth, but Galip was shocked to see how sweaty and bruised Celina was, nearly as pale as the bleached pillows propping her up. Her hair had lost its luster and fell in dark ropes around her face. Black circles ringed her eyes. She looked like she'd been punched in the face. Marshall looked nearly as wrung out himself. He sat on a stool next to the steel-railed bed holding a pink bundle of blankets.

When Galip edged closer, Marshall rose and handed him the bundle. Galip peered at the blotchy little face, a few wisps of blond hair fluffing up from her blue-veined skull.

Her tiny mouth bunched up like a kiss, and Galip pressed his mouth to the soft skin just below her ear. The baby opened her eyes and reached up to Galip, fingers curled into a miniature fist, and hiccupped. Galip's heart ripped open. He'd made jokes about love at first sight when he talked about meeting Marshall, but that was like comparing inches to miles. His legs shook and he practically collapsed onto the stool, cradling the bundle of blankets. "Love should always be like this," he whispered too softly for anyone but the baby to hear.

They called her Amanda Nurai, after Marshall's mother and Galip's mother. "Is that okay with you?" Marshall asked Celina.

"Of course," she replied.

Galip clenched his jaw, holding back the words. Why was he asking her? She was leaving. Wasn't she? But how could Celina let go of this wonder? Because she had a soul of mud, that's how.

One night, after getting up to bring Amanda to Celina for her 2 a.m. feeding, inhaling her scent of powder and milk and just her own Amanda-ness, and then snuggling her warmly back into her bassinette after she was through nursing, Galip spooned up against Marshall and stroked the smooth skin over his high shoulder blades.

Marshall didn't roll over.

"It's been three weeks since Amanda was born," Galip

murmured.

"I'm sorry," Marshall said. "I guess I'm tired tonight." He shifted farther to his side of the bed.

"That's what you said last night. And Saturday night." Galip stared at Marshall's back for a long time before putting his hand out and touching the faint white line of an old scar from his father's belt, barely visible in the moonlight coming through the open curtains. "I need you to tell me what's going on, Marsh."

"There's nothing going on. I'm tired, that's all."

"It's more than that; I know you. You're holding back."

"I told you, it's nothing," Marshall snapped.

Galip rose up out of the bed and slapped on the lights. He circled to Marshall's side of the bed and loomed above him. "I'm not letting you get away with this," he said. "We haven't made love in almost a month, and I want to know what's suddenly come between us."

Marshall sat up and glanced around. "Shh," he said, "lower your voice."

"Why?" Galip didn't lower his voice. "Why should I? Who's going to hear me?"

"Celina will."

"Who gives a damn?"

Marshall leaned forward, gripping the quilt. "I care, damn it. She's the mother of my child."

Galip stepped back. *My child indeed. Marshall never sees what's right in front of him.* Galip should have been furious, but he wasn't. All the anger drained away, replaced by quiet resignation. "So now we come to the truth." He smiled ruefully at Marshall, at himself. "She's the mother of your child. Not ours. Yours. And hers. And don't forget your father, who still hasn't come to visit." He turned from the bed and headed for the closet. "That's always the problem, isn't it?"

"Galip, please, I didn't mean it like that." Marshall appeared next to him as Galip reached for his robe.

"You did, you know," Galip said. "But you're wrong. Amanda isn't yours anymore, or Celina's; she's mine now. I'm the one who loves her. I'll sleep on the couch and see you in the morning."

"I love her too!"

Galip walked past him. It didn't matter how much he loved this man; Marshall would not change. The relationship would not change. Galip had always known that, but it had taken a tiny baby to give him the strength admit it.

"Galip, please talk to me." Marshall reached out to grab his sleeve but managed only to brush his fingertips against Galip's arm. "Yell, scream, throw something," he pleaded. "It scares me when you're this quiet."

"Tomorrow."

When Galip woke, the sky was just beginning to lighten, sunlight slipping pink through the leaves outside the window. He knew what he needed to do. He was completely at peace. All the anger and pain had flamed out and been covered with soot. In the ashes lay dead dreams — to love Marshall, to be loved by him, to belong to him. He should have fought for them, but he hadn't been a warrior then. He was a warrior now. He had Amanda now. In truth, Amanda had him, her tiny fist wrapped around his very soul. He would stay for Amanda.

With small smiles he put off each of Marshall's attempts to start a discussion. He poured them both coffee, handed Marshall his cup, coolly returned Marshall's pressing kiss. Celina watched them, mechanically sipping her protein shake.

"Marshall, love," Celina interrupted, "I was going to ask you about —"

"Oh, do be quiet, the grownups are talking," Marshall snapped, even though they weren't, and headed for the door without breakfast. Celina's cheeks flushed a dull red.

When Marshall was gone, Celina stood to put her glass in the sink and turned to Galip. "Rough night?" Her eyes were slits.

Galip shrugged.

"But then again, I hear you like it rough."

Galip gazed at her, one eyebrow raised.

"The walls are thin, and Marshall and I do talk, you know. After all, he is the father of my child. He said so himself." She smirked, proud of her winning hand.

"Amanda is mine."

"Maybe that's not what a judge would say. I've decided I like it here."

So she wanted more than just the money after all. "You signed a contract. A judge would respect our rights."

"The rights of a couple of *ibneler*?" Celina laughed.

The Turkish word she used carried overtones of disgust and abominations before the Lord. When she said it, Galip heard the thundering rage of his father, felt the thud of his fists, absorbed the guilt of the wild blows his mother took for her part in his depravity. He heard the pity of his sisters, the sniggers of his uncles, the echoes of all the places he would never, ever belong.

But that didn't matter; he was a father now. He flexed his shoulders, accepting the challenge. He would give Amanda everything he ever wanted for himself.

He took a step toward the coffee pot to refill his cup, and Celina took a quick, startled step backward. Did she think he was going to hit her? She shrank away from him, hurt tinged with victory transforming her face, waiting for Galip to hit her. He never would, of course, but she could still skitter off to Marshall with fake fears for herself and their baby. She could press against him and whisper in his ear the fairy tale of what it would be like if only Galip were out of the picture. Had she wanted this all along?

It might have worked at the beginning, but even with a woman in the picture, Marshall's father hadn't come around, and thus Celina was of no further use. She would give up eventually, or Marshall would throw her out; it didn't matter which. She would probably take a few of the jade figurines as she went.

Amanda whimpered and Galip lifted her out of her baby swing, cuddling her against his chest, their breathing in sync. He carried her into the living room and settled down on the couch, the tip of his finger tucked into her mouth. She peered owlishly up at him, adjusting her baby vision.

How hopelessly he had fallen in love with her in such a short time! Amanda, too, would grow up and grow beyond him, blond and beautiful like her biological parents, leaving them all behind. He and Marshall would limp on together, some good times, some bad times, just a normal couple.

One day he would find Marshall's father and tell him exactly what he was missing. All of life, he thought, was a series of eliminations and reductions, tapering down at death to the ultimate vanishing point. But before that, yes, for a time before that, life as Amanda's champion would be fully, completely, utterly glorious. He shut his eyes and sank into the cushions, trying to decide what a knight in shining armor should wear to work.

THE THREE GODS

Once upon a time there was a Poppa God, A Momma God, and a Little God. They were quite traditional in their outlook, as Gods tend to be, so they each had their preassigned role in The Creation.

Because He was the male incarnation, the Poppa God created the heaven and the earth, and divided the light from the darkness. The Momma God told the Poppa God how wonderful He was, and cleaned up after the Little God, who had gotten into the paints. Then She made dinner, and washed the dishes after dinner, and that was the first day.

Poppa God divided the firmament above from the firmament below and called it quits for the second day. "That's it?" Momma God asked. "No stars? No planets? No comets?"

"Okay, stars and comets, but I'm leaving the planets for tomorrow." But then He went back to sleep anyway.

Momma God shrugged and returned to the kitchen to finish the dishes and mop the floor. She also did a load of laundry and clipped Little God's fingernails. She disliked laundry. That was the second day.

In all fairness, Poppa God really did get moving on the third day. He created the dry land and the vast oceans, with a few volcanoes to amuse Little God. He created the mighty forests and the endless deserts, the vines and the grasses. In a burst of romantic sentiment, He added fruit trees and flowers and called Momma God to come look.

"Still no stars, Poppa?" was what She said, but He could tell She was pleased. They went to bed early that night and She left the dishes soaking in the sink.

Poppa God was feeling mighty fine the next morning, so He rolled his big sleeves up and set to work on stars for Momma God. He didn't like making stars because they were difficult to get right, but He made lots of them anyway, all different colors. Then He made the sun and the moon, and the sunrises and sunsets. When He called Momma to come see, She said She was really pleased, and She told him how wonderful He was, but She couldn't stop, She had too much to do. "Besides, Little God is still awake."

So He went back outside and created thunder and lightning, blizzards and tidal waves. "Serves Her right," He muttered.

On the fifth day Poppa God, still sulking, went out with Little God and created stuff He knew She wouldn't like. He created whales and squids and slimy things that live in mud, and plankton and liver flukes and blobby jellyfish. Little God got his pants and shoes wet jumping in puddles and Poppa God didn't stop Him.

Little God was worn out from his morning racing around and took a nap after lunch, so Poppa God decided to be magnanimous and forgive Momma God. "Well, Momma?" he asked.

"Alright," She said.

In the afternoon He created the most beautiful birds He could imagine.

On the sixth day Poppa talked Momma into coming out to create as a family. "I haven't created since I was a little God," Momma protested, her hands white with bread flour. Poppa tickled her until She was breathless and had to give in. Little God stared at them with round eyes.

They got terribly muddy, all of them, and Momma God refused to think about the pile of laundry She would have to face the next day. She watched while Poppa God created cattle and dinosaurs and orangutans. While She was setting out lunch He made cats and koala bears. Then He surprised Her by making a copy of each of them, a Man and a Woman, and She kissed Him.

Little God tried to make everything His Father did, but the only thing He could manage was snakes. After a while He got bored and stuck one on the elephant, and They laughed and left it there because it looked so cute.

"Well, Momma," Poppa God said, looking around at

the result of His labors, "I think this is pretty good, don't you?"

Momma God looked at the filthy clothes, the muddy shoes, and the big grins. She wiped Little God's nose and hoped He wasn't coming down with something. She looked at Poppa God, with His strong hands on His hips, surveying His dominion. "You're a wonderful Creator," She said, Her heart full.

But when no one was looking, Momma God leaned over, scooped up a tiny bit of new earth, and let a single, fragile thought become reality in Her hand. She watched silently as the butterfly emerged from the mud, spread its wings in the clear sunshine and flew away, leaving Her behind. Then She went inside to start dinner.

SERENITY AND SOMETHING PINK

The woman had lived alone in the forest for so long her voice had stopped working. At the start she had talked to herself, then she moved on to one-sided, rambling conversations with flowers and animals. Eventually that eccentricity passed as well, leaving behind the shimmering translucence of a single human, listening.

When she had first left the city behind, with its trains and busses and honking and people rushing and rushing and rushing, everything in this glade had seemed unnaturally silent.

Now she listened to the baby birds shrieking for their next meal, the murmur of roots growing underground, the deep, resonant sigh of glossy leaves stretching for the sky, the ting of tiny berries absorbing the glow of the day. She tipped her head to the wind as it huffed across the garden, the tickle of the clouds as they rubbed against each other, the song of the sun and the melodies of the moon and stars. If she occasionally thought it would be nice to have a hand to hold, a smile reflected back to her, well that was the tradeoff she'd chosen, wasn't it? She listened to the serenity in her heart. *My life is perfect.*

It was astounding that when the traveler arrived, he did so without her knowing. She was crouched in the garden, waiting for the new little shoots to sing out which were weeds and which were herbs, a skill she had discovered to be quite useful, and the next minute he was looming in front of her. She leaped to her feet in surprise. *Where did he come from? And where did he get that shirt?*

He was tall and gaunt and stooped, perhaps with weariness, perhaps with pain. His outstanding feature was his shirt, which was very silky, very large, and very, very pink — the color of peonies blazing in the springtime. "I like the feel of the air around me," hummed the shirt. "I like to bask in the sunshine and gleam in the mist as we travel the world. We have journeyed from dark bars and brilliant parties to monastery retreats and remote tropical islands. Together we have witnessed marvels!"

Well that's quite the fancy shirt for someone so poor. She noted the vagabond's tattered boots and bony wrists. *He must have stolen it.* She studied his pale features. He did not hear the forest speaking to him, she knew. His ears were too full of sound already. He did not even hear that loud shirt. Somehow even standing still he was in motion. His long arms and legs twitched, the hollow planes of his face slanted back and forth as he moved his head, his very breath thrummed, but with the last of his energy. Sagging and tired, he was a clockwork toy running down. The woman thought others probably judged him to be handsome, owing largely to his bright, green eyes and straight, white teeth. *A door or two have opened for that face*, the woman thought. *And a few pairs of legs as well.*

"Hello, my lady." The man swept a courteous bow, doffing his hat. Its long feather trailed through the grass, reminiscing of its earlier life on a partridge that had been moving just slowly enough to make a hot meal one chilly afternoon.

The sturdy backpack on the man's back wobbled, bulging out over one shoulder. "Whoops," it bellowed as the contents tumbled. "Look out below!"

"I am called Tam-Tam," the traveler said. Smoky shadows circled his eyes and he moved with small hesitations. "And you?"

I could answer him if I choose to. The woman crossed her arms over her chest. I do not choose to.

A lock of hair fell across Tam-Tam's forehead, and with a lean hand he pushed it back. She eyed his fingers as they moved, and deep inside, her vocal cords began to hesitantly yawn and stretch, stirring from their long nap.

"If you won't tell me your name, I shall call you 'my lady.'" Tam-Tam laughed, and the sound skittered through the garden and raced off into the distance. "I am a traveler, a wayfarer, a student of field and stream," he announced. "I sleep under the open skies and I eat what the earth brings to my hand. But for just one night, I would dearly love a warm kitchen fire and soft bed with a white feather pillow to rest upon." He eyed her cottage. "What a lovely home you have. Such a clean white. Such warm green shutters. And surrounded by your herbs and flowers." He paused, his face still for a moment. "It's you on the inside, come to the outside."

What nonsense. The woman scowled. And how oddly he talks. His words are all curves, not straight lines. Where does he think he's going with them?

They stared at each other. Then a single word bubbled up from the depths. "No," said the woman, meaning No, she would not offer him those things. She glanced over her shoulder to where her little cottage sat, nestled in the palm of the glade, surrounded by the serenity and protection of the rich, dark forest.

"If you will not invite me to join your table, my lady, I shall invite you to join mine." Again the sound of his laughter bounced across the garden into the trees, chasing the squirrels from their perches. "I shall make you a feast, a symphony of meat and roots and exotic spices from faraway lands. I shall make you my own forest stew, and it shall be the finest you have partaken of."

He's up to something. She raised one eyebrow.

Although I must say he's plenty charming about it.

He lowered his backpack to the ground and rolled up his sleeves. The outside of the cuff was a lighter pink than the inside, as if weathered by the sun, but that was a deliberate effect. "A master weaver in Nepal made my cloth," said the shirt. "Do you see how hints of blue and green reflect from the shadows of the warp and weft?"

The woman glanced around nervously. *This stranger will stomp through my garden and crush my herbs and flowers. He will talk!* She clasped her hands together to keep them still while she decided what to do.

Tam-Tam made an elaborate production out of rummaging through the overstuffed pack. "Hey buddy, watch those hands," the pack snapped, shoving the edge of something sharply forward. Tam-Tam jerked his hand back. The woman pressed her lips together to hide her amusement. Tam-Tam had quite nice hands. He shoved up his sleeves and reached back into the pack.

Out came a dented, tarnished pot. "Oh dear," sighed the pot, "is it that time again already?"

With a triumphant grin, Tam-Tam displayed the pot as if it were a great treasure. "Now where are those spices? Hmm, I think I'll use cardamon, cinnamon, maybe ginger as well. And peppers, of course, for bite." He looked up at her from where he crouched, his gaze intent. "Because everything in life needs a little bit of bite."

"As long as you don't lose control of it," she said, refusing to back up in the glare of his smile. It was the first full sentence she'd spoken in a long time. *Is that what I sound like now? So rusty!*

He glanced at her in surprise, nodded without comment, and rummaged through the pack again.

"Okay, okay, here," it snarled, shifting a lumpy pouch into view.

"Now we need a good place for a fire." Tam-Tam swiveled with dramatic flair as he studied his surroundings.

The woman panicked. A fire? In her forest? Burning the leaves and the grasses that sang to her each morning? She couldn't tolerate the thought. She had to stop him. "No," she croaked again.

Tam-Tam stopped. The woman paused as well. What to say next? If she told him to leave, he would merely go just out of sight, where she would still hear him. Where she would still feel him setting his flames crackling in her forest.

As much as she hated to make the offer, it would have to be her kitchen hearth after all. She squared her shoulders. He was searching for something, and she emphatically did not want him finding it at her hearthside. But she had no choice, so as her heart thumped, she turned and led the way.

"Your home is every bit as welcoming inside as outside." Tam-Tam spread his hands before him, inviting her to join in his appreciation. Wooden surfaces gleamed with polish and care, cups and plates and pots shone in the soft light, a single chair with puffy cushions faced the large fireplace.

He's surely up to something, she thought again. She monitored his strange movements with narrowed eyes.

"Oh, this is a much better pot than mine, it will make much more stew." He put down his own pot, which promptly went back to sleep, lifted her middle-sized pot, the one with the shiny copper bottom, and filled it from the pump over the sink. He stoked the fire and settled the pot in place. With a fanfare of body movements, he dropped in a pinch of his exotic spices, a handful of dried herbs smelling mostly of rosemary, and a few scraps of dried meat.

Together, they contemplated the ingredients lying at the bottom of the pot. Small bubbles formed around and under the meat, rose to the surface, popped with tiny noises that made the woman twitch. "It is boiling very nicely," she forced out.

"Yes, it is. Of course, it has been scientifically proven that water boils faster if a bit of salt is added." The woman crossed her arms over her chest again. They both knew she had salt, it was in a bag in the cupboard, but she was damned if she was going to give it to him. Besides, water did not boil faster with salt in it. After another few minutes of staring at the water, she began to feel ashamed of her stubbornness. It was only a little salt, after all.

When she handed him the bag, he grinned at her and winked. She quickly looked back at the pot. It was only a pot of water with some salt and the start of a weak stew, but she had liked his wink. "It smells good," she creaked, even though it didn't really have much smell at all. Well maybe a bit.

"If you think it smells good now, you should smell this stew when it has the harmony of onions and garlic to accompany its melody."

Oh ho, so that's his game, she realized. She tapped her foot in smug irritation, but in the corner of the room, under the sound of the bubbling pot and the surge of Tam-Tam's breathing, she heard the vegetables ripening in their drawer.

How green his eyes are, she noticed when she handed him the strings of onions and garlic. With sharp, sure movements, Tam-Tam sliced them into moist circles and dropped them, one at a time, into the simmering broth.

A froth rose to the surface and he stirred it back down with the point of his knife. "To make it a little thicker," he told her.

"I like thick stew."

"I do too. I am particularly partial to a forest stew thickened with barley."

Well he's stuck there, I don't have any barley, I only have wheat berries. A smile curved her mouth. Tam-Tam smiled back, as if he knew exactly what joke they were sharing. Then she remembered she had cracked those wheat berries just last week, so they would be at their best right now.

As long as she was in the pantry, scooping the wheat berries from the earthenware crock, she took some carrots and early tomatoes out of their baskets. For color.

When she realized what she had done, she gathered other ingredients for a thick stew, handing them to Tam-Tam with a rueful laugh.

Tam-Tam added more pinches of this and pinches of that, tasting and adjusting.

She set the table with the best china and silver, opened the one remaining bottle of last year's summer wine and sliced the loaf of bread she had baked that morning. *He might think he's conning me, but he's not.*

She combed her hair, when she thought he wasn't looking.

"Oh Lordy!" The small table groaned under the unaccustomed weight of such a meal. Bowls of stew steamed at each place, fragrant and inviting. Slices of bread sprang softly away from the cut of the knife. Butter, pale as moonlight, waited its turn on the delicate plate. The wine in the glasses sparkled and chuckled in the firelight.

With the food spread out before them, they filled the little cottage with a merriment that drowned out all the other sounds of the night and forest outside. Tam-Tam recounted wicked and amusing tales of his adventures and the people he had met. The woman shared gentle stories of the captivating songs of the tiniest woodland insects. He told ribald jokes, she tried not to laugh and failed. *I have been missing this. A companion for my days, and a story that isn't mine.* Each mouthful of stew filled her with the warmth of rich flavors. Each swallow of wine made her bolder. Her voice sprang forth, limber and clear, in a rush of tumbling, teasing swirls.

"Where did you get your shirt?"

"I'll never tell." He grinned at her, long and hard. He breathed as if he had not inhaled deeply in a long time. He reached for more bread and more stew. He ate as if he had a hole inside him he was only now beginning to fill.

"If you don't tell me, I'll hide your pack."

"If you hide my pack, I will have to stay until I find it. I cannot travel far without it."

"Then I won't take it," she said, retreating rapidly.

When the meal was over, they settled back, quietly sipping the last of the buttercup wine, chasing stray crumbs with idle forefingers.

"Now, my lady, how about that soft bed with the white feather pillow?"

"Your shirt makes me nervous," she confessed.

"I had been planning to remove it."

"I think you've stolen it."

"In a manner of speaking, I did." He reached for the buttons on the front.

"I know what you're up to," she told him.

"I find it's better that way," he replied.

She relearned many sounds that night, sounds she had not heard in a long time. First came the shiftings and rustlings of their clothing as they helped each other to undress. Then came the squeaking and groaning of the bed as they lay down and began to move against each other. At last the first, long harmonies and melodies of their passion and joy filled the cottage and the night beyond. For once the forest creatures were quiet. It was their turn to listen.

In the early dawn the woman opened her eyes to find Tam-Tam watching her.

"Good morning, my lady," he said, and touched a hand to her cheek. "I had a such an enticing dream last night. I dreamed I made love to a princess, and she made love to me in return." He pulled her to him. "I think I must still be dreaming because here before me is that very princess. Come to me, my princess."

She went to him, awash in his words. "Stop talking and kiss me." She tipped her face up to his and drew his mouth hard against hers, relishing in the pressure of his lips and the demands of his body. Their breath and energy mixed into song, their colors and sounds merged into flight. She arced and cried out, as did he, and then they settled, damp and warm and soft, against the soft bed with the white feather pillows.

The morning was growing old by the time the woman awoke again. She lay snuggled in the crook of Tam-Tam's shoulder, one of her arms tucked under his ribs. She listened to his heavy breathing, watched his chest rise and fall. Outside in the garden, the rabbits stained their noses purple with ripening berries. A bright, white cloud swished by, giggling at the sight, calling to her. A doe tiptoed up to the window and peered in. The woman tried to listen to the sound of her happy heart, but her mouth felt fuzzy and her fingers were going numb. She shifted her arm ever so slightly and Tam-Tam woke.

He sat up in the narrow bed and stretched his arms high over his head. The shadows were gone from his eyes and his shoulders were straight and square and strong. He smiled at her, bright and joyful. "You make me feel magical." He turned his head intently, as if he could finally hear the voices all around him. He perched naked on the edge of the bed and pulled her into his embrace. "It's as if everything in the world has come to life."

"Perhaps it has." She tried to smile as she leaned away from him. There was so much of him! So much skin, so much hair, so much color, so many smells! She rolled away and wrapped herself quickly in her robe. His shoulders were so very large!

"I could stay."

Time stopped. She had left the world behind once and been glad of it, in her fashion. Now it had come to find her, she had a chance to change her mind. Did she want him to stay? She thought of Tam-Tam in her garden, his strong hands working the soil, his smile as they harvested the fruit. She thought of sleeping beside him every night, holding each other close and warm. Sharing thoughts. Sharing hearts. He would give up his traveling to stay with her. She would need to give up her serenity. She would need to give up herself.

"I," she stumbled over her words, "I cannot." She felt the relief of a firm decision verbalized. "You cannot either."

He let go of her and stood. "Then my journey lies ahead of me." He reached for his clothing.

"The wind and the waves are calling, calling," sang the pink shirt as it rippled over his shoulders.

"Strange sights to see, new people to meet," chimed in the trousers as they slid up over his hips.

"Each new day is a shining new road," agreed the stained and tattered boots.

"Awright, we're outta here," crowed the backpack.

"I could use another night's rest," the little pot whispered.

They dawdled over their breakfast of porridge and raspberries, even while the woman sneaked glances outside at the warm, rich colors of the fields and forest. At last Tam-Tam picked up his pack.

"You are welcome to come back if you pass this way again," she said.

"I don't often return to a place I've already been, no matter how special." With a final kiss, he turned and walked out of the door.

She waved him on his way, watching him gradually blend into the forest. When she could no longer see even a hint of pink, she practically danced outside to tend her garden. Last night had been extraordinary. Not just the physical intimacy of course, but the laughter, the conversation, the tints and hues of companionship. Everything they'd shared had been so full, so abundant with color, so rich with new voices. Her mind swirled with remembered sensations and all around her the world seemed a little more colorful, and little more sweetly perfumed. She settled down to tend the spikes of summer seedlings, her ears, her eyes, her mouth still full of Tam-Tam and his spicy presence. She reveled in the light friction of cloth against her newly sensitized skin.

She listened intently to the gentle songs of her world. The bright summer field flowers sang lightly, birds in the tree nearby — no longer babies — trilled in reply.

Everything was serene, if a little subdued, now that Tam-Tam was gone. The colors and scents settled into the placid swirl of her life in the clearing, in the garden, in the forest.

A knot of rose madder had invaded the garden and she yanked at it, falling backward with its sudden release. The root was nearly the same bright pink as that shirt. *Tam-Tam's shirt.* Knowing she would never see him again was a waterfall, cold and sudden, dousing her.

"He came here weary and hungry, needing to rest, needing safe harbor, and then just walked away!" She stabbed her fingers into the dirt. "I didn't want him to stay, I told him to go." The eager garden sounds faded and the vivid colors slunk off to the forest where that pink dot had last been seen. The trees swayed in the wind, sounding dull and ordinary. "I am not diminished by what I have given away. I am enriched by what I have shared."

Well doesn't that just sound stupid, she thought, her voice receding to her chest.

She nearly destroyed the delicate thyme by yanking it; only the squeak of crushed leaves alerted her to her mistake. *I'm better off without him. If I must choose between too much noise and too much silence, I'll take silence, thank you very much.* She patted the damaged thyme back into the dirt. *Not everything with bite is good.*

She worked long and hard the rest of the day to tire herself, to lull her muscles into the rhythm of the earth, to still her angry pulse drowning out the humming of the peaceful forest, the chime of the sunlight ribboning down through the leaves into the clearing, the whispered splashing of warmth spreading over garden. The day passed. She rubbed her hand across her face, leaving a streak of ordinary mud behind. The bruised thyme hummed gentle forgiveness. As the sun settled down behind the edge of the wood, she rose to her feet and returned, aching, toward her cottage.

A bit of bread, a bit of cheese, and a night of soft dreams, she thought. That's all I want right now. My life may not be perfect, but it's right for me. It may feel flat now and then, but that is my choice. My tradeoff.

It caught her eye as soon as she stepped through the door — how could it not? — a glaring splash of pink. It smelled of Tam-Tam; his scent opened its arms to greet her. He had he come back. It didn't matter that he had left again, it was enough that he had returned with this gift. Having done so once, he might again someday, bringing his energy, bringing his fire, bringing the pain of knowing he would always leave. She shut her eyes and inhaled deeply. She lifted the shirt and shook it out in front of her. Its folds and weave glimmered in the twilight, its colors dancing as it rippled through the air.

"You have seduced me away from the road, I will

relish the wondrous stories of the quiet forest. So many new stories to discover!" it yodeled. "So many old stories to uncover!"

"Tell us, tell us," begged the little stool by the fire.

"Yes do," chirped the littlest pot, "tell us, tell us."

The woman laughed as she slid the soft fabric against her skin and whirled around the room, lifting Tam-Tam's fragrance into the air. *Not tonight. But on a cold night, when a warm fire isn't enough, when serenity is too small, then it will be glorious to have new stories to share.* She draped the shirt carefully over the back of the chair by the warm fire.

The Werewolf of Sander's Notch

The cold burn of our hike through the woods made the air in the Blackney's dairy barn feel warm and close. I jumped and twisted as shadows reached out for me then shrank back. Doug's flashlight, swinging into distant corners, created movement where there was none and I had an unsettled feeling in the pit of my stomach, like smelling ozone before lightning hits. I was sure we were going to get caught, if not by Mr. Blackney, then by bats or mice. What would people think of me, a third-grade teacher responsible for setting a good example, caught trespassing in the middle of the night?

I clung to Doug's hand, struggling to breathe the moist, heavy air, ripe with the odors of manure, hay, and old timber. The heifers in their stalls stamped and snorted quietly, drowsing in the dim light. "I'm scared," I said. My voice sounded loud in the stillness. Suppose the old journal Doug had found in the basement of the library had been right? Suppose there really was a werewolf, generation after generation of werewolves, that came out to feed under the light of the full moon? I immediately felt foolish, it was silly to be afraid of my own imagination, but I touched Doug's extra hunting knife hanging from my belt. Why had we decided not to bring a gun?

Doug squeezed my hand. "We'll be fine, we just need a safe place to hide." His voice fell cold and cheerless on my spirit. Was there ever a good place to hide from a monster? "I think the corn crib will do," he said, indicating the high bin against one wall. "Hold the camera while I get in." From the tone of his voice, the lurking dangers of this night had gotten into his head too.

As a hiding place it might be adequate, but it surely didn't look too comfortable. I balanced the old, infrared camera on my leg and watched while Doug swung gracefully over the top railing. He has beautiful muscles, I thought distractedly. I tried to stomp down those disturbing thoughts. One of the things I liked best about our relationship was its tranquility, its freedom from emotional highs and lows. A scrabbling noise nearby made me jump. The corn in the crib was dried cobs, not fresh. Broken bits and ends poked my face and dug through the down of my ski jacket into my arms and chest as I burrowed deep for cover. I sneezed several times from the dust before I managed to stretch the neck of my sweater up over my nose, trying not to think about mealy worms and rats.

I wasn't proud of my cowardice. I struggled with my

lack of courage, knowing it was not too late to go home. It wasn't as though I had a reputation for bravery to protect; I had never been known for my courage. Nightmares had haunted my childhood. Visions of muggers and rapists, and the noisy, dirty hustle of the city streets, had led me to turn down a prime teaching job in Boston and take one in the tiny village of Sander's Notch. It was tedious and it didn't pay well, but it was only nine miles down the road from where I lived with the elderly aunt who had so carefully raised me, and five miles from where Doug lived with his parents.

I had touched my toe in deeper waters once, and had then snatched it back from the shadowy, swift moving depths. His name was Tony and he was twenty-five, an experience man when I was still a virgin of twenty-two. His dark, lean looks made my blood tingle as soon as he arrived at the party, with a friend of a friend from the other side of town. We ended the evening in his bed. As the passion inside me woke, so long held in check by my old-fashioned upbringing, I panicked. The fires I had never allowed to surface threatened to overwhelm me, and if I let them out once, I knew I would never be able to jam them back in. Unable to face that, I had run, never looking back.

"You work so hard being safe and dull," a friend had kidded. But I liked the image of myself as a cool, calm, and rational young woman with a sensible job and a logical approach to life. I liked the idea of my life stretching out smooth and calm ahead of me, disappearing into the placid, blue distance. As for Doug, others might call him boring, but he suited me just fine. Except for his preoccupation with this nonsensical werewolf story. I had only come on this expedition to humor him and I was regretting it now.

The silver gleam of moonlight visible through chinks in the old barn told us the full moon was rising. I peered through the wooden slats of the corn crib and tensed down in the corner, waiting in silence for the monster to appear, sweat chilling on my skin.

An hour later I was still there, topid with boredom, neck muscles aching from the constant swiveling side to side. Two hours later I was more than ready to leave. My fear had given way to scorn, it was ridiculous to be cowering in the barn of a perfectly ordinary New England dairy farmer. "Let's get out of here," I whispered. "I'm stiff, cold, and this is a stupid idea. There's no such thing as werewolves."

"You saw the diary."

"I saw the notebook of some old crackpot who was probably hitting his own still a little too hard. I've taught in this town for three years, I've met all the Blackneys, I've had the kids in my class. They're no more werewolves than I am.

"Let's wait a little longer." Doug shifted position slightly and I felt the corn shift around him. "Please?"

"The camera probably won't even work after burying it in this dust," I grumbled. "I'm bored and I haven't the faintest idea how you talked me into this."

As I was about to declare myself fully out of there, the heavy door of the barn creaked on its hinges and started to swing outward. The moon was high overhead, painting the snowy scene outside with a luminous blue glow. In the clear light I could see as far away as the stand of pine on the other side of the pasture. A large creature moved around the edge of the door, huge paws rasping against the ground, shallow claw marks furrowing the hard dirt.

Every hair on my body stood straight up. Sweat flushed my skin and my breath locked in my lungs. The corn cobs that had been digging into my ribs no longer bothered me at all.

A drawing of a dangerous animal in a book is no comparison to being faced with the real thing. My mind fought, rebelling at the thought that here, in front of me, was proof of something I had been taught all my life to deny. I tried to convince myself that what I was seeing was a normal, natural inhabitant of the night, a stray cow or a common black bear. But I knew, deep down I knew I was lying. Less than twenty feet away, even in this dim light I could see the massive muscles rippling along its shoulders and back as it stalked forward with primal grace. I watched its thick fur ruffling in the soft wind from the open barn door. It was close enough to touch. Was it close enough to smell me? My skin tingled. One deep breath and I would be discovered. I wondered if my brain would be conscious of my body being torn apart.

And with that thought came the realization that my death no longer hovered safely distant but faced me here. Tonight. *Dear God, please don't let me die tonight.*

The werewolf slid over to the row of cow stalls and unlatched one of the doors with its thick paws. Doug and I huddled there, buried in the corn bin, frozen in horror as the creature dragged the screaming, lowing sacrifice into the shaft of light spilling down from the moon. The lover's moon. The snow moon. I watched every move the beast made, hypnotized by the silver highlights thrown back from the curves of his solid haunches, the angles of his grasping jaws. *Dear God, please don't let me die tonight.*

The agonized howling of the terrified heifer stopped with shocking suddenness as the werewolf ripped through its throat. Blood sprayed black against the straw, the stalls, the carcass of the falling cow. Splatters came as far as the bin where we crouched and I struggled to stay still, not to draw back further into the corn. The beast began to eat with slobbering gusto, the fur on its paws and face matting with blood and entrails. Gobbets of meat and flesh straggled down its chin onto its chest. It devoured the scraps and crunched the bones. Time came to a standstill as the feast went on.

Steam rose from the warm cavity of the recently living repast. Sour acid rose in my throat but I couldn't look away. My breath scissored up and down my throat in short, silent stabs. A thrumming pulse sounded in my ears. Within the cocoon of my revulsion, this unrestrained savagery buffeted me as if by physical touch.

The beast made a noise deep in his throat, as if it were humming. Its tongue, shining wet in the darkness, slowly licked a drop of blood from the corner of its lower lip and my mouth grew warm. I leaned forward. Raw sensation came leaping, tumbling, catapulting up from the depths of my gut. Something deep and slumbering inside of me, something made of fur and fire, began to wake. I could hear Doug struggling not to vomit and I strained to recall the shape of his placid, gentle face, without success.

A sliver of noise, a tiny soft sound caught my attention. A small child stood poised at the entrance to the barn, sharply outlined in the silver light. An edge of lace trailed from the hem of her nightgown, looking impossibly delicate in the dirt under the heel of her winter boot.

No! I wanted to cry out. *Run! Run!* But I stayed frozen, my heart thudding in my cowardly ears. I had just this night come to life —I had just come to see that my life was more than the organic chemistry of my cells. Must I relinquish it so soon? I wanted Doug to move but I knew from his jerky breaths that he was as terrified as I.

Surely the child would see the beast right in front of her before it turned and grabbed her! Surely she would recognize the danger she was in before it was too late! But still she moved forward, into that hunger, unaware of her fate. Her toe caught against a stick and the slight crackle sounded like gunfire in the night. The beast peered up from its kill, a haunch as large as the girl herself dropping from its paws. Its humming noise ceased as suddenly as the cries of the heifer had.

I wanted to move. I wanted to leap forward to put my body between the monster and the child, but my terrified limbs refused. Its gaze riveted on the girl, the beast opened its wide jaws and let out a mighty bellow, a howl that made the corn around me vibrate and the wooden slats of the bin tremble under me. Anger was in that creature's cry, and a depth of longing that roused an answering ache in the marrow of my bones. My fingers cramped impotently around the hilt of the hunting knife.

Still the girl moved forward.

I reached deep inside myself to that secret place that had terrified me so long, waking the sleeper faintly stirring there. I knew the danger I was in, I knew that this awakening was one I would not return from, but I could not sacrifice the life of that child to coddle my own fears. I would not sell that child's life for the price of my own.

In that understanding I found the strength to move. I found the courage to burst through the mass of corn above me, knife clutched in one sweaty hand.

But the girl had reached the dreadful monster, huddling over the remains of its midnight feast. "Mom says you're to come in now."

The beast crouched over the meat and snarled, the noise covering the crash of the corn slithering as I aborted my rescue. The upper railing of the crib caught me in the stomach, knocking the breath out of me as I struggled for silence. The cobs at my knees trembled as Doug remained in hiding.

The girl put one arm around the neck of the werewolf and hugged hard, blood smearing her jacket, and her face scrunched up with a grin. "I know, Daddy," she said, "but Mom says you've had enough." The creature hunkered down and growled again, more softly. "Mom says now." The girl was insistent in her mission. The beast growled once more, in defeat.

The child slipped one hand into the fur on the beast's neck as it pilfered a last morsel. "Come on, Daddy, or Mom'll come for you herself. She's going to be mad when she sees the mess you made this time."

The beast took a swipe at the girl's face with his huge tongue and she laughed and hugged him again.

I stood frozen against the railing, nakedly exposed to

the most casual of glances, trying not to breathe, my attention riveted on the beast and the child. Sweat ran down my back. The smell of blood and wet fur enveloped me. I was aware of the tiniest details of life around me. I was going to live! In a few moments they would leave this barn and I would be free.

Then the beast raised his great head. Perhaps he was only longing for the few succulent bits remaining. Perhaps he had known all along I was there. Our gazes locked, an eternity in a single moment. I saw his amusement at the futility of my gesture, and his understanding, as I held the puny knife aloft, prepared to protect his daughter. Within our gaze the beast in him met the beast in me eye to eye. Then he turned away, and together they went off into the moonlight, a little girl in a white nightgown leading a lumbering beast with bloody fur.

The night was quiet and dark again. I dropped the knife and climbed over the wooden slats. I inflated my lungs with the heavy air, exhaled slowly, while my new intensity filled me. I don't know how long I stood, savoring the rush of life through my veins, exploring the richness of my own being. The imps that had always chattered away at my nerves had fled, vanquished. I was huge, savage, towering a mile high over the mortal world below me.

"It's alright, you can come out now," I said to Doug, still hiding, three feet and a whole night away from me. I had shed him as completely as I had shed myself.

I would shrink back again in time, of course, but never again would I fit inside those boundaries that had once wrapped so safely around me. And sometimes, when the moon was full and silver, I would relive this night. How strange that such a pivotal moment in my life had taken place here, among straw and corn. How ironic that my life, stretching out ahead of me in panoramic possibility, should be the gift of a creature known for death. And yet, how fitting.

In the path of the moonlight, the gutted carcass of the heifer was a black velvet testimonial, and I wondered what teaching positions were open in Paris. I suddenly longed to fly away to Paris and eat chocolate with my hands.

ANOTHER SATURDAY NIGHT

Mary Frances Theresa O'Halloran settled down heavily on the couch in front of the tv. Another Saturday night alone. She hadn't been able to muster the energy to swipe any of her dating apps, so no date, no friends who were not out on a date, nothing but tv or a video game and a bottle of Sabra to keep her company. Sabra was her booze of choice. It was a little sweet, downright syrupy in fact, but she liked chocolate, and she liked oranges, and the bottle appealed to her. Broad based, with a narrow neck, etched in blue and gold with Hebrew runes, it was made in Israel but looked like something a genie would pop out of. She reached to refill her glass, realized the bottle was empty, and levered herself off the couch to get a new bottle from the kitchen. Returning to her seat on the couch, Theresa struggled with the top for quite a while before loosening it. It seemed to be held on much tighter than usual.

Quite suddenly the top was in her hand, the bottle was on the floor, and a genie was indeed popping out. Or smoking out, rather, with very little noise and fuss. Theresa jumped to her feet and watched, heart pounding, as the smoke slowly swirled and condensed. Before her eyes a bent, white-hair Hassid, complete with black coat, straggling sidecurls, dangling white fringes, and a furry, round hat. She opened her mouth and goggled.

"And just what are you staring at?"

"You're … you're … you're …"

"I'm what?" the old man snapped. "I'm a genie?"

"You're a Jew!"

"This comes as a surprise? What did you expect from a bottle of Sabra, Chris Hemsworth maybe?"

"Well, I, ah," Theresa swallowed. "I thought a genie would be big and broad, and bald, with a gold earring." Theresa heard herself babbling.

"You want Vin Diesel, drink Schlitz." The old man turned to the door, brushing some dust, or smoke, off his coat. "Well, been nice schmoozing mit you, but now I go."

"Hey, wait a minute." Theresa snapped into focus. "I thought you were my slave now, your wish is my command and all that."

The genie looked at her with disdain. "Forget it, no deal. I'll go back in the bottle." He began to smoke a little around the edges.

"No, no, don't go. How about three wishes?"

The smoke got thicker, the old man got thinner.

"Two wishes."

The genie stopped fading, but remained half smoke, half matter.

"One wish then, one wish and you can go," Theresa made her final bid.

The old man reappeared with a snap, straightened his fringes and heaved a great sigh. "What is the world coming to when a nice girl like you would try to cheat a poor old man like me. How many wishes you think I got left at my age, hmm?"

Theresa folded her arms across her chest.

"Alright, one wish. Just one. Go ahead."

Theresa closed her eyes and thought of all the things she might wish for. Beauty? A bottomless bank account? Fame? Talent? Success?

"Come on, you think I got all day to stand here?"

"I want," she paused, hesitant to put her deepest desire into words. Unsure of how to put her desires into words. "I want a man who will love me forever and think I'm the most wonderful person in the world and who won't think of anything except my welfare and he should be tall with black hair and blue eyes." She spoke in one breathless rush. "And Catholic, of course," she added hastily.

"You call that one wish?" the genie sneered. "He should maybe have the moon in one hand and a mink in the other?"

"You said one wish, and that's what I want." Theresa stood firm, refusing to show how much he intimidated her.

"I just hope you appreciate how much work for a wish like that."

"I do, I do," she assured him.

The genie sighed again, then turned around three times and raised his hands to the ceiling. The lights in the apartment began to dim as the old man rocked back and forth in his shabby shoes. Clapping his hands in front of his chest dramatically, he recited:

> *Mishooganah shiksa,*
> *oy veh, vat a goy!*
> *She wants her dear bubbeh*
> *should turn into a boy.*

He clapped his hands once more and a crack of thunder shook the apartment, deafening Theresa and knocking the saltshaker off the kitchen table. By the time Theresa had recovered her breath, the genie was gone, taking his bottle with him.

But the person who had materialized in the center of the living room was still there. He was indeed everything she had wished for, he was tall, blue-eyed and dark haired. He took her in his arms, kissed her on the top of the head and said, "You look terrible, are you coming down with something? Are you eating right? I'll bet you've been staying out drinking and smoking until all hours of the day and night, you'll kill yourself at forty, just like your grandfather, that lazy good for nothing that he was." He hugged her again. "But I'm here now, and I'm going to take good care of you."

The next morning, Mary Frances Theresa O'Halloran, groggy from a dawn breakfast of fried eggs, fried potatoes, fried bread, and oatmeal with cream, and leaden with a feeling that something had gone horribly, terribly, dreadfully wrong with her wish, stopped in at the office two doors down the hall from hers.

"Bubbeh?" Sarah Levin said, "I don't speak that much Yiddish, it's kind of old-fashioned. I think it means grandmother. Why?"

THE RAINY SEASON

The old woman passed the liquor store and slunk up to the battered '69 Chevy, animal instinct guiding her to the warmth of a recently used engine. She would have been content to huddle near the pale comfort of the hood of the car, but discovering a door unlocked, she struggled over the door frame and went to ground on the floor in the rear. She pulled the door shut behind her, curled her ankles under her, and wrapped a tatter of cloth over the scabs on her thighs. Strings of hair that had once been brown, or perhaps blonde, slithered across her face. All that remained of the once human potential were sharp, ice blue eyes flicking furtively out through the folds of skin and the mists of madness.

The November rain beat cold and relentless in this empty section of Tenth Avenue. The old woman discovered a blanket crammed under the passenger seat, pulled it over her head, and settled gratefully into the security of her new home. What did she dream of there in her shabby cocoon? She had certainly been a child during the hungers of the

Great Depression, she must have been a teenager during the Second Great War and a young woman during the bountiful Fifties. Would the layers, unwrapped, reveal a first love dead on a beach in Normandy, the bodies of two grown sons returned, half rotted, from the jungles of Dien Phu?

Two men in jeans and down jackets with ski masks pulled over their faces raced out of the liquor store and leaped into the front of the car. Within seconds the car was in motion, tires protesting against the asphalt as the driver slung the vehicle into the street. A speeding taxi honked in protest and veered away. Rain splattered the windshield.

The passenger leaned forward in his seat, gripping a canvas bag against his crotch and jerking his head from side to side as the car turned to merged with the traffic on the cross street.

"Wow man, what a rush!" he exclaimed. "Did you see the blood?" His eyes gleamed in the flare of the oncoming headlights and his chest heaved.

"I saw it. You better hope he ain't dead, asshole." The driver didn't move his eyes from their steady attention to the wet street and the other traffic crossing and weaving in front of him. "You get worse every time."

"He was an old guy. Who gonna miss him?"

The driver shook his head but said nothing. He wheeled the car around a tight corner, heading downtown. "Get yer damn mask off, Joey," he said, removing his own.

He was the older of the two, with a weary look that whispered of too many nights like this, too many small dreams lost. He was squarely built and dark, and his hands on the wheel held the car in firm, conscious control. "Oh man," he said, rubbing his nose, "what's that stink?"

Joey kept one hand on the bag and pulled the wet mask off with the other. Lank, brown hair fell across his pale forehead. He sniffed the air loudly. "Smells like you shit in yer pants, Rick. Action getting too much for you?" He threw the driver a mocking grin.

"I can handle the action. You probably stepped in some dog shit back there."

"Did not!" Joey made an angry chopping motion with his hand. But he glanced down at his feet when he thought the other wasn't looking. Rick caught the movement out of the corner of his eye and smiled quietly. Joey, noticing the smile, flushed dark. He stared rigidly out through the windshield, watching the raindrops trying to crawl upwards against the glass and the wipers beating them back down. The slap, slap of the wipers punctuated the steady moaning of many tires on wet pavement.

"How much do ya think we got?" Joey asked after a while. "Can I count it?"

"Sure. Knock yourself out." The driver glanced from the road briefly. "Just don't think you can slip none of it into your pocket while I'm not watching."

"Come on, Rick, you know you can trust me," any guilty thoughts blanketed with a steadfast look of practiced innocence. But his eyes sparked with mutiny as he studiously bent over the bag in his lap, his lips moving as he thumbed through the bills. Light from the thousand passing sources streaked across his face and hands. "Nearly eight hundred. Fuckin shee-it!"

"Shit is right," the older man muttered with disgust. "I was expecting more like fifteen."

"Well I ain't never seen this much in one piece before, not bein' a pro like you," Joey sneered.

"You ain't got that much now, either," Rick reminded him, "Two thirds of that's mine."

"Yeah, yeah, I know." Joey settled back with a sulk. "This time," he muttered. Out of Rick's line of sight, he made a finger gun and aimed it at Rick. Pulled the trigger.

Once again conversation ceased and the impatient sound of cars fleeing the city moved in. Joey stretched out a hand and flicked on the radio to a loud beat.

The old woman in the back levered herself onto the rear seat and tipped her head back, eyes shut, oblivious to the men in front.

Rick glanced in the rear mirror to check the traffic and slammed on the brakes in startled reaction.

The old woman slid to the floor.

Joey swung around, gun in hand, and fired one shot

wildly in the direction of the back seat.

"Fuckin' A," Rick yelled, and jerked the wheel with a curse, sending the car in a half sideways slew toward the curb. Horns blared angrily in response but avoided the erratic vehicle, which slammed to a stop with two tires crushed against the sidewalk.

Rick spun around, pulling his gun out as well. He leveled it toward the woman but spoke to the other man. "You're a fuckin' maniac, Joey. You're gonna get us both killed." He took a few breaths, then spoke to the woman, who had risen back up to the seat. "Who the hell are you?" he demanded.

She looked blearily at the guns facing her with no sign of interest, her gaze drifting randomly to the sparkling raindrop on the window by her head.

"I said," Rick lowered his voice to chilling level, "who the fuck are you?" He nudged the muzzle of his gun against her forehead. Joey wriggled and touched the tip of his wet tongue to his lips.

A glimmer of fear flicked in the woman's eyes. Rick jabbed her in the forehead again. "What's your name, you old goat?"

"She sure smells like an old goat," Joey said. "A shitty old goat."

The woman swallowed; her lips moved. A trickle of saliva appeared at one corner of her mouth. She appeared aware that she had not actually said anything, because her lips moved again and this time the response was audible. "Rosa," she creaked. "They calls me Momma Rosa."

"Okay, Momma Rosa, what the fuck you doing here?"

"Please mister, I just wanna get outa the rain." Gummy blue eyes looked up at Rick prayerfully. Sudden recognition lit there. "I know you," she exclaimed.

Rick moved slightly and his grip on the gun tightened just perceptibly.

A coy grin lit the woman's face, flashing a hint of what might have been beauty at least one world war in the past. "You're Bobby Bowen," she announced. "I knew you looked familiar." She paused, and wriggled slightly more upright, the filthy blanket slipping just a bit off one shoulder. "Don't you remember," she prompted, "we met at Sally Mitchell's house party last month?"

Rick relaxed. "Yes," he replied with a nod. "I remember. You gave me the first waltz."

"Yes, a waltz." The momentary alertness faded. The grey, greasy head swiveled back to the raindrops.

Rick stuffed the gun back inside his jacket. Joey looked at him with a smirk, his own gun still out and cocked. "Sweet little love scene, *Bobby*."

"Shut up, Joey. She's just a crazy, old lady." He looked out the window at the sheets of rain. "Fuck. We're gonna have to screw around dumping her somewhere she can't get back from real fast."

Joey stared at the woman and flexed his shoulders. "She's no harmless old woman, she's faking it." He drew in a breath through parted lips. "Let's kill her."

"Cool it, asshole. And put your gun away."

Joey held his gun out a little straighter. "No one would miss her. Be like shootin' a rat." He leaned forward, arching his back like a prowling cat.

"Somebody would find the body, it ain't worth the risk. And we're not doing it." Rick eased his hand up toward his jacket, keeping his eyes on Joey.

"She's faking it," Joey insisted, "look at her eyes. She just wants you to think she's nuts so you'll let her go." He moved the gun another inch closer. "We don't have to do it here in the car, we could take her somewhere quiet and make it last."

"I can't believe I stuck with you this long," Rick said. "After this I'm done with your bullshit and trouble." He whipped his gun out of his pocket and pressed it against the young man's temple, "We ain't gonna kill her. We're leaving her somewhere alive. Now put that thing away and let me think."

Joey hesitated. "This is a mistake," he said, but tucked the gun carefully back in his jacket. He appeared to settle in his seat, but he had the look of a hungry animal behind bars.

"We'll take her over to the piers," Rick announced.

"No one for miles around on a night like this." He put the car in gear and eased back onto the street, one hand holding the gun rock steady. The traffic steadily thinned as Rick made his way to the waterfront. One by one the streaming headlights and taillights disappeared, leaving them to travel alone.

Under the pier, the pavement was dark with oily puddles in spite of the sheltering overhead structure. The air stank of dead fish and snails washed up on the rocks below the guard fence. The continuous chewing of water against earth muffled the sound of the running engine.

Rick stepped out of the car and opened the rear door. With one hand he reached out for the old woman. He didn't appear to notice the slow movement of the young man, his slightly drawn breath, his tense silence. "Come, my lady," Rick coaxed, "I believe I have this dance."

"Why, of course you do, Bobby." Momma Rosa tipped her head to one side and smiled with missing teeth, a sudden dimple gracing her grey cheek. She allowed herself to be handed out of the car, taking his elbow perkily as they walked toward the pilings.

So slowly, so quietly, the front passenger door opened. Joey eased out of the seat, shielded behind the door panel, his gun ready. Around the corner of the door he took careful aim, a ripe smile curving his lips as if he could taste his target.

It was all over quickly. Alert to the other man after all, Rick swung around and fired two shots. Glass exploded backward over Joey's body as it fell to the cement behind the car door.

And then, quite quietly, accompanied only by the sound of the river below, Rick's body was falling to the cement as well. Momma Rosa stood above him for a minute, wiping blood and rust from the broken tip of an old fishing knife. She looked at the bubble of blood in the open throat and the question in the terrified eyes. "You're nasty scum, Rick, but I guess I can spare a quarter to call the cops." She sighed. "It used to be a nickel."

Two hours later she rose out of the subway exit into the sludge and warmth of the Port Authority bus terminal. The tall, skinny Black man in the mangy mink stole and the broken silk top hat shrieked when he saw her. "Hey, Momma Rosa! Come here and tell the Stork where you been in this suck awful weather."

Momma Rosa veered slightly to join him leaning against the wall. Shifting her layers of rags and blankets around her, she eased down onto the floor. "Been sliding on a liquor store job I lucked into. Two mean shitheads." Her head shook in wonder at the poison in the world.

"Wow man, sliding. Not for me, man," the Stork said. "Every two-bit punk out there's got a handful of bullets and a gut fulla mean. Most of 'em are nuts." He scratched an sore on his bare thigh. "There's easier ways to make a buck, even in November."

Momma Rosa shrugged, her face impassive. "You do what you gotta, man. You do what you gotta." Then her face crinkled and a harsh laugh sounded from her chest. "Besides, what's the fun if it can't get ya killed?

How to Catch an Elf

S o you want to catch an elf of your very own, do you? I suppose you think that having one is cool because that actor fellow has one. Or because you think that hot redhead in your Comp Sci class will be impressed, and she isn't impressed by much. Trust me, having an elf will help about as much as borrowing your grandmother's car.

You don't believe me, do you? You're a dope. Go away, I don't want to talk to you anymore.

Why are you still here? That determined, are you? You're still a dope. And you can't just go into the nearest elf store and buy one, have you thought about that? You're going to have to catch it. Yourself. With your own two hands. Have you any idea even how to begin?

Oh, that's why you're here, is it? You didn't come to visit an old, senile professor in his musty lair because you desired the wisdom of the ages, the chance to learn from one who has devoted a lifetime to the never-ending pursuit of all knowledge, following the path of learning the unlearnable and searching for the answer to the ultimate mystery. You came because you want to get laid.

Yes, thank you, a little more of that whiskey would be just fine.

Well, you know what? I'm going to tell you what you want to know. I hope you get what you think you want out of it, but more than that, I hope you stop hanging around and bothering me. If you succeed, just maybe you'll learn something. You can't catch an elf if you don't understand yourself a little bit. Heh, heh, the little fellows are probably pretty safe.

Are you ready? Put that stupid notebook away. If you can't remember simple directions, you don't have a rat's chance of succeeding in this.

Now then, there are two basic ways to capture an elf. If you don't count the time old Mortimer Sheridan caught one by tripping over it, drunk, in the dark. The elf was drunk, I mean, not old Mortimer, although he'd probably had a snootful as well, knowing Mort. But I don't think you can count on that technique, although you're welcome to try. Punched Mort in the crown jewels, too, as I recall.

Now, where was I? Oh, yes. Two methods. One requires physical strength and stamina. Hmm. I wouldn't advise that one. One requires personal charm and style. I'm not sure I'd advise that one either.

If I were you, I'd spend my time studying, get into dental school, and convince your redhead that you're going to be a good provider.

No? I knew you were a dope. By the way, you only have one chance, so you'd better be right the first time, because if you fail in your first attempt, the elves will always be wary of you.

Well then, let's get started. If you choose to capture your elf using your brute strength, the first thing you have to do it build a trap. Elves are not stupid, and they will not get caught by crude traps. They will not fall into holes in the ground covered with leaves, they will not crawl under boxes propped up with sticks, no matter how many brownies you put there. You wouldn't happen to have any brownies with you now, would you? How about cashews? I do like cashews. Except when they get stuck under my bridge. Are you sure you don't have any? Oh well.

What's that? Me? I've found the best thing to do is shape and paint a burlap sack to look like a gingerbread house because elves are mischievous and love to go in and tease the witch. Set up your trap in an open clearing in the woods, in the daytime when all the elves are sleeping. If even one of them gets wind of what you're doing, he will tell the others. Yes, yes, or she. Tie a string to a corner of the house, hide in the woods with the other end of the string, and wait until night falls. Don't fall asleep.

When an elf goes in, pull the string and *voila!* one elf, all neatly tied up in a burlap sack. If you're strong enough to carry an angry, struggling elf all the way home, you're set. Did I mention that elves can bite through burlap? Did I mention what he's likely to do to you if he gets out of the bag? Yes, yes, or she. I wouldn't give short odds for your future with the redhead after that.

Of course, if you're not that strong, this method is not for you. Perhaps you can rely on your, ahem, charm. Elves are susceptible to the magnetism little children, so disguised as one, you can win the heart of an elf in no time Dressed in pink and white lace and lots of ribbon, crawl out to a clearing in the woods. Just as twilight comes, shake your rattle and start to cry.

This will draw the attention of several of the little people, who will come to play with you. Most will soon get bored and drift off, but one will get stuck with the chore of minding the human kid, and this is your elf. Mind you, he's going to be pretty cranky because he missed his dinner, and in all likelihood, a decent poker game.

Now start crawling slowly toward your house, playing and cooing to keep his interest. When you get home, crawl in the front door — did I mention you have to leave it open so you don't blow your cover now? Once inside, start to cry again and the elf will come to see what's wrong. Then you can jump up and shut the door, capturing the little guy. Of course, now you have a hostile elf on your hands, with no burlap between you and him. Yes, yes, or her. This is where your personal charm will come in especially handy.

Of course they both sound difficult. They are. Dental school, that's the ticket. Yes, thank you, just a splash more. Well, I wish you all the success in the world, now go away.

Hello there, back so soon? Two weeks already? How quickly time passes when the mind is blissfully occupied by the joyous pursuit of the unknowable. Have you trodden one small step on the road to the infinite? You look like hell, you must have been successful. Having an elf around the house is not at all what you thought it would be, is it?

Been complaining about the food? The color of the bathroom? He rearranged your underwear drawer because you didn't have it right?

Well, how about that hot redhead in your Comp Sci class? Did that at least work out the way you wanted? Was she impressed by the elf?

Really? She's sleeping with him? Or is it a her?

EXCERPT FROM
WHERE THE RIVER BENDS

CELESTE

When the police arrived at Celeste Vandenholm's door that dismal November afternoon, at the end of that dismal year of 1930, her first thought was *Oh God, Peter has found out about me.*

But Peter hadn't found out, and later Celeste would wonder why she had even thought that. It would make no sense to think the police would be involved. *Perhaps.*

The older officer took off his cap and held it against his chest, his fingers brushing pellets of sleet off the stiff brim. "I'm sorry to tell you this, ma'am, your husband has been in an automobile accident." The younger officer solemnly nodded.

Celeste didn't hear a word after that, other than "hospital" and "operating."

The whole day splintered into a kaleidoscope of

disconnected fragments from which she tried to snap into action: ringing for Timmins to call a hackney, standing like a stone statue while he opened an umbrella for her, bitter, salty spray catching her in the face as one of the new Ford roadsters sped down Park Avenue.

"New York German Hospital," she instructed the driver, striving to be strong, confident, in control.

"Yes, ma'am," he'd said. "They call it Lenox Hill now," he informed her conversationally. "They done renamed it, must be ten years ago now." He glanced at her in the mirror and fell silent as they drove on, the wheels whirring against the wet pavement.

She had rushed to the hospital, but now the wait was endless. Waiting to be shown to the waiting room. Waiting for Peter to come out of surgery. Waiting to find out what was happening. Waiting for her thoughts to stop whirling so she could pray.

"The first day after any surgery is the most critical," Dr. Stegmann said, when he finally arrived. He wore a clean surgical gown, but a single streak of vivid scarlet crossed his cheek.

That's Peter's blood. Celeste turned her head, trying not to see what she would never forget.

"His wounds were extensive, but we managed to stop all the bleeding, so that's good news." He took her hand and pressed it gently. "But he also has a fractured skull, and three broken bones in his neck. We won't be able to tell how much brain and nerve damage there is, until he wakes up."

It took a moment for the words to make sense. "When he wakes up?" Celeste could barely choke out the words. "When will that be? When will he wake up?"

"We don't know. All we can do is pray it will be soon." He touched her hand. "The nurses will be bringing him up from the operating theater in an hour or two."

Celeste wanted to collapse onto the floor in agony, but had no recourse but to wait and then wait even more.

At long last someone ushered her into what seemed to be an absurdly comfortable hospital room. She stepped blithely through the doorway, and suddenly there he was, shockingly close enough to touch, not even an arm's length away. She jumped backward, startled, and cried out. Bile rose up and for a moment she struggled not to vomit right there. She gouged her nails into the back of her neck, concentrating on the pain until the dizziness passed, then she took a short, but infinitely long step forward and gripped the sheet lying over Peter's arm. She was barely aware of the nurse moving a chair up to the bed for her, and she sank into it without letting go of Peter. The nurse murmured a few words about calling if anything was needed, then closed the door behind her.

Celeste put her head down on the railing next to Peter's face, listening to his faint breathing. At least he was still breathing, she could cling to that. So many nights she had lain next to him, reaching out for sleep that didn't come, while he dropped into slumber like a rock into a pond, then flopped around onto his back and started to snore. "Roll over, honey, you're snoring," she'd say, shaking him lightly, marveling at how the dim gaslight caught the clean lines of his cheekbones.

How would she live if anything were to happen to her Peter? "Please come back to me," she whispered. "Please."

He didn't wake up the first day. It was an entire day, wasn't it? She couldn't recall.

She remembered calling Briarwood Academy and asking Headmaster Hibbeler to put David on a train for New York.

She remembered calling home, and asking Nurse Savener to explain to Martina that Father would not be able to play chess with her that night. Martina's addled, confused mental condition would not be able to grasp the situation, but perhaps she was the fortunate one, in that regard, at least. She'd been that way from birth, in spite of all the doctors tried. Who knew what she thought about anything?

Hospital staff in white uniforms bustled up and down the hallway in a blur; one of them brought her a cup of terrible coffee with a thin film of oil floating on the surface, and offered her a sandwich. Celeste shook her head. Fear and anger surged through her in alternate waves, ebbing and flowing, like the ocean against the shore. She huddled in the hard chair and waited for Peter to wake up.

Half of his face was mottled and swollen with bruises; the other half was hidden behind bandages that had once been white but were now streaked with blood. He lay motionless, arms at his sides, raised up on pillows, trapped inside a cage of bed railings. The electric lighting cast a peculiar matte look to his skin, as if he were made of a strange, oddly tinted clay.

"Oh God, oh God, why?" she whispered, and bent over once more, clutched the sheets and tried to pray, but it had been a long time since she'd believed that God was an old man with a white beard who stepped in to rescue every puny human in pain.

She rested her face gently next to Peter's. He didn't move. That was the worst part — he simply didn't move. He didn't reach out to stroke her hair, he didn't put his hand under her chin and kiss her, as he always did when she was upset. He was simply gone. This is what Momma had looked like when she died, this eerie, forbidding sense of emptiness, of unknown danger lurking out of sight. Momma and Peter, these were the people who were supposed to keep her safe. Now everything was the wrong way around and she was utterly lost.

"Are you in pain?" she whispered. "Please don't be in

pain. Please just come home. I need you to come home. The children need you to come home." She clamped down yet another surge of tears.

"I didn't lie to you on purpose. I just always loved you too much to tell you the truth."

ABOUT THE AUTHOR

E lissa Matthews was born and raised in New Jersey, close enough to visit New York City and watch the turmoil of Civil Rights, Women's Rights, and anti-war demonstrations firsthand, then return to the quiet of the country to absorb and understand. Her short stories deal, in one way or another, with our lies, our masks, and the issues we need courage to face.

In addition to the many short stories and poems published in literary journals, Elissa has one novel. **Where the River Bends** is the story of a Black woman passing for White in New York in 1931, and the cataclysm of events that occur when her family finds out.

You can contact her through her website:

www.epmatthews.com

A Request from the Author

Thank you for taking the time to read my book - I hope your time (and money) were well spent. I would greatly appreciate hearing your review, either on *Amazon* or **Goodreads**. Even a few sentences or a rating helps an author grow on their journey as a writer.

Sincerely,
Elissa Matthews

132

Acknowledgements

Over the many years I have been writing (and rewriting and rewriting) these stories, so many people helped me on the way that I can no longer count them. The support of the vast, quiet community of writers, editors, teachers, librarians, and especially readers who keep the art of story alive is worth more to me than I can express. There have been so many individuals I can not name them all here, but some of you have stood by me, brainstorming, critiquing and cheerleading, for decades.

To Ruth, Alan, Pam, Mary, JR, Nev, Judy, Elaine:

I am forever in your debt.

www.ingramcontent.com/pod-product-compliance
Lightning Source LLC
Chambersburg PA
CBHW072304130726

47910CB00012B/2430